SCARED
MONEY

MARK CRAMER

City Miner Books, Berkeley

Creative Services: Penn&Ink
Production Services: Graphic Page
Design & Layout: Dayna Goforth Schippmann
Cover Design: Sandra Page Taylor

The author would like to thank Bill Conklin, Martha Cramer, Stan Gutkowski, Bob
Fellows, Mike Helm, Pennfield Jensen, Ron Mitchell, Nick Setka, Dick Stone and
Gary Williamson for their critical readings of the manuscript.

Library of Congress Catalog Card Number: 94-68302

Published by City Miner Books
P.O. Box 176, Berkeley, CA 94701

ISBN 0-933944-15-2

Printed in the United States of America by City Miner Book

10 9 8 7 6 5 4 3 2 1

for Martha,
my partner in love and calculated risk

PREFACE

I recall an impassioned confession from a corporate executive.

"Mark," he told me. "I'd gladly dump my job for the race track if I could only make a portion of what I make at work."

While numerous horseplayers have already made this unconventional choice, even more continue to lead a double life, maintaining their position in the straight world but dedicating an intense portion of their existence to improving their game. Unlike the hard-core cynics found in most popular racing fiction, these are gutsy romantics who truly believe the races can be beaten. They cannot be pigeonholed by age, sex or profession. Often with family responsibilities, they must daily find that delicate balance between their struggle to beat the odds and their desire to fulfill a role in society.

Thanks in part to the popular cliche of the degenerate horseplayer, however, anyone trying to become a winning player must first psychologically overcome the scorn heaped on them from society at large. *Scared Money* is about the passionate dream of becoming a pro, of building the self-confidence necessary to prevail in a game where 98 percent of the players habitually get beaten.

Though horseplayers are bombarded with systems and methodologies that promise to make them winners, the truth is that even some of the best handicappers are psychologically conditioned to lose.

The stories that Matt narrates in *Scared Money* confront such vital psychological issues as dealing with losing streaks,

1

relating to loved ones, avoiding dependency, overcoming deep-seated cultural taboos and building self-confidence.

The fictionalized setting here, based on predicaments any good horseplayer can relate to, hopefully will allow readers to experience, rather than being told, what they must do to confront the ultimate enemy within.

Not only horseplayers but anyone who has ever contemplated abandoning a predictable life in favor of one based on calculated risk should appreciate Matt's sometimes hilarious often complicated struggle towards realizing himself.

—Mark Cramer
Saratoga, 1994

"Experience is the worst teacher; it gives the test before presenting the lesson."

—Vernon Law, former pitcher
Pittsburgh Pirates

SCARED MONEY

McCarron's horse began to shorten stride. I wanted the finish line to get to him from in front before the Delahoussaye horse got to him from behind. Judging from the primal screams of the players around me in the Hollywood Park grandstand, their lives depended on the outcome of this one horse race.

I wasn't there exclusively for therapy, however. I wanted to make my living at the track, and that involved looking at the races by the month, by the quarter and by the year. If McCarron didn't manage to hold on, I had other races. It was still better than a day at the office, I reassured myself.

From one perspective, the Delahoussaye horse was shooting by like a bullet. But that was an optical illusion. In reality, the McCarron horse was slowing down. The finish line didn't quite get there on time. My horse lost by the bob of a head. I gave myself thirty seconds to recover and it was on to the next race.

My wanting to be a professional horse bettor was not merely a choice of the spirit, it was a virtual obligation. Sure, I had my piano gigs. I was even playing with a former bassist of Ella Fitzgerald! But my economic future in the world of jazz was subject to marketing considerations external to my own skills. At the races, it was all up to me.

Because of my background, straight jobs were hard to come by. Shrewd personnel officers would find suspicious items in my application, that I was born in Medellín, Colombia, for example, and that I had an M.A. in music. Those two pieces of data correlated into the probability that I

5

was part of a drug culture. No reputable company was prepared to bet on me.

My father, a Colombian-born physicist, had insisted that my name be Matthew, as opposed to Mateo, over the objections of my mother, a New Yorker of secular Jewish background. They had met during my mother's two year stint in the Peace Corps.

My father's argument was based on logic. His future was in the United States, doing research. He wanted me to fit in. Why erect a potential barrier to my success with a Spanish name? His Catalan last name, Bosch, was generic enough to be safe from stereotypes.

My mother, a piano teacher, had argued that the sound of Mateo was both strong and sensual, with a musical curl at the end. But my father won.

Had he been alive and with me today, seeing the McCarron horse lose by a nose, he would have admonished, "You see, Matt, the odds are against you. When will you get on with a more practical profession?"

But the path to professional well-being was strewn with larger obstacles. My anglicized name couldn't make up for the dubious reputation of the city on my birth certificate. Had my father anticipated the drug stigma attached to "Medellín," he would have paid off a local bureaucrat to alter my birth place from Medellín to Popayán or Bogotá.

Brenda, soon to be my ex-wife, had taunted me on my inability to land a straight job. But to the corporate world, I was like an illegal alien. My Latin features, including the dark eyes and straight black hair did not help.

So music was one of the few avenues open to me and I had now reached a professional plateau, playing mostly pop-jazz with a house band at The Money Tree, in North Hollywood. I was part of a trio—my piano, with bass and drums, with the club occasionally bringing in a guest vocalist to add another dimension.

Meanwhile, I hoped that the restraining order would keep

Brenda from stalking me at the club where I played, or at the race track, the other place where she knew she could find me. In Brenda's mind, every female in a jazz club audience was my potential lover. She would eye them all, then make sure there were no groupies waiting around for me after the last set. She was jealous of my music, too, and jealous of any horse that I "loved" on the day's card.

The restraining order, the regular income from The Money Tree, and my impending divorce should have released me once and for all from the grinding tension of my past life. The living ruins of my past, however, did not wither away. I was paying the mortgage on the house in Culver City, where Brenda and my two kids lived. I was making monthly payments on a piece of land she had purchased as an investment. I had a divorce lawyer to pay. And I was blackmailed into covering for the Rodeo Drive boutique debts Brenda had spitefully run up on our credit card, since my own credit was at stake.

She had also kept the good car. I had the Ford, which was okay by Blue Book standards but teetering on the edge of collapse as a result of a previous accident. "*Her* previous accident!" I emphasized to no avail at the deposition where the cars were meted out.

When I got to my apartment on Vermont Avenue that evening, there was more bad news in the mail. Inside the business envelope was a court date that threatened to further deplete my meager bankroll. At issue was the amount of my child support payments. I was now employed. Brenda only worked part time. I was already behind on my rent. If she won the extra child support, I'd be out on the street.

Outside the courtroom, on the appointed date, my attorney prepped me. The fact that all our debts were a result of her bad judgments was not admissible as evidence.

Over the indifferent objection of my attorney, Brenda managed to sneak in the fact that I was a horseplayer. Naturally, Judge Mary Doyle had read Damon Runyon and assumed that all horseplayers are social misfits who squander their income on the ponies.

7

I whispered to my lawyer. The fact that I kept records, I said, distinguished me from the majority of horseplayers. I could present a ledger that would prove to the judge that I had made a small profit for the year. A very small profit, but, hey, I wasn't a loser. He too must have read Damon Runyon. He told me to bury the subject, that we didn't want to attract any more attention to my horse betting.

Neither strategy would have made a difference to Judge Mary Doyle. Since I had money to bet on the ponies, she reasoned, I could well afford to pay more child support. Case closed.

Judge Doyle was responsible for a milestone in my life. Then and there I resolved to prove that horse betting was a respectable profession. In order to achieve my goal, I would have to accelerate my plan for becoming professional. But the first rule for horse betting, "Don't play with scared money," was standing in my way. I had $76.28 to my name.

The next day, I informed the property managers that I would be moving out on the first of the month. I didn't tell them that I would be moving into my Ford.

In fact, I had an elaborate plan worked out so that no one, not even my closest friends, not even Samantha, my new girlfriend, would find out I was a *"sin casa."* The "H" word sounds less demeaning in Spanish. I'd get off work at three in the morning, drive to a nearby restaurant parking lot on Camarillo, then sleep in the car. I'd be awakened by the morning rush hour traffic, hit the ignition and swing down to Valley College over surface streets, where I'd use the restroom facilities.

I developed a sophisticated method of sponge bathing, whereby I would soak a bunch of paper towels, some of them in liquid soap, some just in water, take them all into the toilet stall, out of sight, then bathe and rinse.

Once freshened, I would doze for another hour at a library desk, then study the Form for the day's races. Working at night allowed me the luxury of betting by day.

On the way to the track, I'd sometimes stop off at Monica's house. Monica was the only person alive who knew I had no home. Since she didn't know any of my other friends, I didn't care. Besides, Monica was that rare kind of casual friend with whom you can come clean with no misgivings. She made it easy for me, by sharing intimate details of her own life based on her reverence for Anais Nin.

Monica even gave me the key to her apartment so I could keep my clothing there, as well as sleep and bathe in the morning after she left for work.

But most of the time my pride did not allow me to take advantage of her generosity. So the Valley College system was the core of my curriculum.

Bad as my economic plight was, that didn't stop me from regularly making it out to the track with my tip money from the previous night's gig. But if the race track were to save me, I quickly realized I'd have to overcome my greatest weakness: betting too many races. Intellectually I understood that a true edge does not arise in every race. But psychologically, it was difficult to stay out.

With virtually no bankroll, "scared money" would have been an improvement for me. I was a couple of notches below scared money. I didn't have enough money to be scared to lose. The irony was that when I was playing scared, I'd prefer to bet less money on more races, instead of focusing on those few races where my insight went beyond the trivial.

Hollywood Park, of course, is in Inglewood, a bad neighborhood in the public perception. Since parking and admission at Hollywood Park would deplete my already miniscule bankroll, I was forced to park my car on side streets. In a moment of inspiration, I got Raul, the manager of the Money Tree, to advance me some salary, so I could add theft insurance to my auto policy. I then parked on the seediest street of Inglewood, leaving my car door unlocked, hoping with a little luck the thing would get stolen so I could collect on the insurance.

Meanwhile, I got into the track with the help of Jake, for only a buck. Jake's job made you love the free enterprise system. He would pay his admission, then get his hand stamped on the way back out to the parking lot. He would tell the brothers approaching the ticket gates that he could get them in for a buck. He would then moisten the stamped part of his black hand with saliva and press it firmly onto the correct part of his client's hand. The client would now have a stamped hand, allowing him to saunter in for free.

I became Jake's most faithful client. Sometimes, when business was good, he wouldn't even charge me. I figured he'd make about fifteen stamp transfers until the ink had worn off, then he'd pay another three-dollar admission and start the process all over again.

Saving on overhead did not prevent me from underperforming at the betting windows. I was losing two dollars here, five dollars there on marginal bets; by the time my best race came up, I wouldn't have enough left for a decent score. In races where there were two or more contenders, the fear of losing made me play the most likely winner at lower odds, even though my second or third choice might have offered a much greater betting advantage.

Days went by, and my car was not getting stolen. I decided to enhance the chances for a successful insurance investment by leaving the keys in the car. The only moral qualm I had was that I might be responsible for entrapment. What if the kid who eventually stole my car was caught? A kid would do time and it would be my fault. Still, statistically, I rationalized, that was unlikely. The cops were not going to waste their time on the automobile of an unknown jazz musician.

Another week passed and still no one wanted the car. I tried parking it on different streets, in the shadows of eucalyptus trees, in front of liquor stores or next to empty lots. There were no takers.

In the meantime, it was becoming more difficult to conceal the fact that I was *sans toit*. *Sin casa*. Homeless. I came to realize that my homelessness was affecting my self-image.

Self-image is more important than handicapping when it comes to making a profit at the track. Guys with low self-esteem tend to be bad decision makers. They press. They fear betting against the crowd. The only way for a player with the wrong approach to change his habits is to change his self-perception.

My secret was eating away at me. For the first time in years, it began to bother me that I was only five foot seven. And instead of feeling the usual surge of energy from hearing Thelonius Monk, his eccentric piano solos would now make me doubt my own talent.

Had I mentioned my homelessness, my friends might have understood. But deep down inside I feared they would lose a piece of their respect for me. The only good thing about the street was that I could park anywhere, out of reach of my stalking ex-wife. To her, I was a hard-core unemployable, a deadbeat father, a degenerate horseplayer, and yet, strangely she would do anything to get me back.

Then there was hot and sassy Samantha, my new red-headed squeeze. The stats said that Sam would dump me as soon as she perceived my new identity. She was from a class-conscious Beverly Hills family. Out of rebelliousness against her family, she had married early, divorced, and was now working as a mini-skirted waitress in a swanky, high-tip restaurant.

It seemed only a matter of time before she asked why I no longer invited her to my apartment. Still, I couldn't take the risk of telling her. It came down to a sense of honor, my old man's code of honor. Although he had lived a universal, cosmological existence, beyond culture, within him had remained this code of honor, a vestige of Golden Age Spain. One must maintain appearances. Appearances are more important than reality.

It struck me as odd that a modern physicist at the Fermi Institute could harbor these antiquated hangups, yet the code of honor held firm within my father until his dying day, and evidently had been passed on to me. I didn't accept this code intellectually, but I soon began showing up at the club in a suit and tie. Anything to cover up my secret truth. Curtis, the bass player, was the first to suspect.

"Whoa Matt," he'd say. "You goin' through some big changes, huh? What's this suit-and-tie shit?"

"Just fittin' in with James," I equivocated. James was the drummer, an old-timer who once played with Ella and came to work looking like a Wall Street broker.

"Don't be jivin' me, Matt."

"Hey, if Little Brother Montgomery could suit up every night, why can't I?"

Curtis and I had both grown up in the Hyde Park neighborhood of Chicago, within blocks of each other, although he had a few years on me and our paths had not crossed at that time. I knew about Montgomery, the famous blues musician, because he had rented a flat in my building. I would have latched on to him as my first guru, had he not lived in such a detached world. Montgomery's suit-and-tie routine was his way of distancing himself from the young hippie blues artists who played on Chicago's North Side.

A few days later, the Ford died, succumbing to irreparable internal problems. The stereotype about the young black male residents of Inglewood, California had proven incorrect. I was now in deep trouble. I'd have to bus it, which was another blow to my self-esteem, since mainly down-and-outers took buses in L.A. In New York, stock brokers and book editors used public transportation. But in L.A., dishwashers and Salvadoran cleaning ladies took the bus. There were also lots of folks who talked to themselves on the bus. Mutterers. And men who could have been hired for shaving commercials to exemplify the deficiencies of the Brand-X razor. I had nothing against these folks. But at this precarious time of my life, their presence was no boost to my self-esteem.

Meanwhile, at least I had my regular lunch dates with Samantha. They were on Mondays and Tuesdays, dark days on the racing calendar. We would make love, brunch on red wine and cheese, then make love again. She worked the night shift. It was a perfect arrangement.

Sam lived near La Brea and Wilshire, near the Tar Pits, on a street lined with lanky palm trees. I arrived there with a briefcase, which concealed changes of underwear and socks, all the while debating whether or not to tell her of my plight.

But, Sam was no dummy. There were too many pieces of evidence by now. My phony excuses for not inviting her to my apartment, my disconnected phone. And now, I had no car. She knew about the exorbitant child support payments. She knew about the mortgage, the land payments and credit card debts. Surely, she knew what was going on but didn't want to press me.

"Look," I finally said. "You might have guessed by now. I've hit rock bottom."

I dodged the word "homeless." So did she.

Surprisingly, Samantha wasn't turned off by my homelessness. For her, it was the Christian thing to help those in distress. She seemed to like me more now, not less. She gained strength from my predicament. She relished the role of protectoress of the downtrodden. Instead of being demoted a few notches in her estimation, I had received a promotion.

"I believe in you," she said.

If she could believe in me, why shouldn't I believe in myself? In a rare moment of self-assurance, I made a flash decision. I would attack the races, scared money or not, this time with the right attitude. The race track would lift me off the street.

The next person to figure out my secret was Curtis. He, too, offered his home to me. But he warned me to cut out the self-pity.

"*Your* problem is finite," he said. "I'll introduce you to some homeboys who got no way out. Then you won't be feelin' sorry for yourself."

He lived with his wife and ten-year old boy in a vintage 1926 three-bedroom wood frame house in South Central, the type that had the old plaster-and-lath walls. Modest, but safe in an earthquake.

With the truth out of the bag, my life had simplified in some ways; but in others it was more complicated. Some of my clothing was at Sam's, some at Curtis's and the rest at Monica's along with my keyboard, which was gathering dust. I often dressed in geographic stages. When I ran out of shirts at Curtis's, I bussed to Monica's for a clean one.

When the horses moved to Santa Anita, all my connections had to be renegotiated. Samantha, basking in her noblesse oblige, said that she'd like to introduce me to her folks. She was getting serious and that scared me. She was Bunuel's Viridiana, harboring a romantic notion about street people while I knew there was nothing romantic about bathing in toilet stalls with wet paper towels.

Meanwhile, Monica had acquired a live-in boyfriend and needed more privacy. Her place was now off limits. Curtis's house was two and a half hours by bus to Santa Anita. The safety net I had worked so hard to weave was unwinding.

My only hope was the race track. I needed my own wheels to get there regularly. A valid address was the prerequisite for my purchasing a car on credit. An apartment would have to be my first step off the street. But in L.A. they required first month, last month and a deposit. This move-in money functioned like an immense moat around even the shabbiest of two-floor stucco walkups. I had now saved enough from my gigs to pay a modest rent. The move-in money was holding me back.

My best chance for the move-in was a big score at the track. Going out there every day was a drain. Up a few bucks one day, down the next, I was getting nowhere. I needed to be more selective. In a moment of lucidity, between sets at The Money Tree, I came up with a plan.

I decided to confront my most serious weakness, the inability to pass races. This was not going to be a final resolution of the problem, but it would be a step in the right direction. I needed to put at least fifty bucks into one race. I needed to wait for that race. Perhaps wait out a whole card of racing. Maybe pass two or three days until the one ideal race came along.

I would be looking for a race in which the two "logical" public choices could be totally eliminated. That would leave me with only longshots. I would be required to narrow down my contenders to three or less. I would go for the throat, a $15 exacta box of my top two choices, and ten buck exactas with top choice to third choice and second choice to third choice. If the odds were spectacular, I might consider win bets, too.

I needed to clear at least a thousand in order to move into an apartment. If there was ever a scared money bet, this was it. My back was to the wall and I would have only one chance. This scenario was begging me to break down and split up my bankroll into small bets among several races.

The ideal race appeared on Thursday's card. It was the fourth, a turf event. The favorite was trying the grass for the first time and was bred to hate it, a mare by Bolger. The second favorite was stabled with a no-win trainer and was hung out in the outside post position; at the mile distance, beginning before a turn, she'd go wide.

Only three fillies had legitimate turf breeding, Nijinsky's River, Northern Prancer and Arch Diesis. They were all trying the grass for the first time. The rest of the field either had proven to dislike the grass or had bad turf breeding.

I got there just after the first race. The smog had lifted and the craggy San Gabriel Mountains behind the backstretch were glistening in the sun. Several of my friends were up in the M section. But any human contact at this moment might remind me of my homelessness, thus impairing my decision making. I'd find my friends some other time, after I had an apartment, when I was less vulnerable.

I went to my favorite perch, high up at the end of the grandstand, above Clockers' Corner, where you have the best view of the most strategic part of the race, the turn for home.

The crowd was compressed near the finish line. I was alone, near the head of the stretch.

The first hurdle of the day was to pass the two races prior to my big event. I could have put ten or twelve bucks into each of the preliminaries, on the notion that a mere $2 exacta box could offer a substantial payoff. The temptation usually gets to you when you look down at the past performances, then look up at the toteboard and see some seducing odds. Passing races was never easy for me. What devastation of the spirit if I chose the winner at a huge price in one of these preliminary races and didn't bet?

There were all kinds of rationalizations for deviating from my plan. But this was a business plan. If one day I would ever have the chance to become a pro, then the least I could do today was to stick with that one race where my insight transcended the banal fixations of classic handicapping.

I needed an alternative activity to distract me from the two races I was supposed to pass.

There was a tap on my shoulder. I wanted no distractions, not even from friends. I panicked. One of my friends had found me. Larry, or Nick, maybe. I turned around.

It was Brenda, all dolled up with a frizzy new hairdo.

My heart galloped out of control. My eye of the storm had vanished.

"Matt, what's happening? I've been trying to reach you. You're phone's disconnected. The kids are worried."

Sweet and sour Brenda had pressed the sweet button. The fire from her dark eyes had subsided, as it occasionally would. Her features had softened and elongated, from the hard-boned lines of a Roualt to the serenity of a Modigliani.

Fugitive Richard Kimble, on being spotted by Sergeant Gerard, could not have felt more threatened than I did at this moment. With no home and no car, pride had not allowed me to visit my kids. That left me vulnerable to Brenda's raids on my peace of mind.

"Do you need a place to stay?" she asked. "I can set you up in the garage. I won't bother you. Remember, we have a sofa there. You could have your independence."

Some independence. The restraining order in my pocket was a worthless piece of paper. An angry response would only drive her back to her usual self, setting off a potentially violent scene. I needed to humor her. I needed to get rid of her well before my crucial betting decision. Already, my objectivity was seriously threatened.

I remembered Monica's sage advice. "Next time Brenda stalks you, say something that catches her off guard."

"Brenda," I said, urgently. "I'm glad you're here. Lend me some money. I have a good horse in the sixth and I'm out of cash."

Brenda liked to bet a horse from time to time. She grinned.

"Who's the horse?"

I opened my form to the sixth race. I looked gleefully for the most-likely loser. I picked out Ingenuous, a proven loser in the maiden claiming ranks, trained by Hal Bryant, a no-win trainer.

"Thanks, I'll bet him myself," she said.

I had pressed the right button and she had changed her channel. I piled it on.

"Well, you be sure to give me 20 percent of your winnings," I prodded.

She got up from her chair, for a moment looking down on me in a way I didn't like. I stood up.

"I'm going to leave you now," she peered at me. "But I'll always know where you are! And I don't care about any goddamn restraining orders. I can check up on you any time I want."

She grinned again. In a matter of seconds, her facial features went back 20,000 years in the evolutionary calendar. She strutted away.

Between that moment and the first flash of the fourth race, I waited in the men's room. Strangely, as a result of the disturbing encounter, I had lost my urge to bet the two preliminary races. My meager bankroll would be intact for the big race.

I splashed cold water on my face from time to time, while considering all my possible betting strategies. The smell of shit was a great improvement over the stressful confrontation that had just ended. I couldn't shake the fear that Brenda might be waiting for me outside that bathroom door.

My decision-making skills might have been seriously sabotaged by now. I glanced out of the bathroom doorway. No Brenda. I went out to a dark corner where I could see the odds for my race on a monitor.

I repeated my mantra; "content determines form." The content here consisted of three longshots, all above 10-1, with Nijinsky's River the longest, at 30-1 because of her terrible dirt races. "Form," or structure, is the way you manage your money. With the tote board odds as a guide, I realized that the longshot "content" of my handicapping dictated that I put more money on the win and less on the exactas than I had planned. Fortunately, I had borrowed an extra twenty dollars from Curtis just in case.

I decided to bet early, while my thoughts remained relatively lucid. I shied away from any complex permutations and kept it simple, betting $15 to win on each of the three longshots, then a $4 exacta box of all three, for a total of $69.

I watched the race on the monitor, in a nook under the grandstand, where even Brenda might not find me. Nijinsky's River, offering the highest payoff of all, was leading around the first turn, into the backstretch. The other two ran midpack. As they rounded by Clockers' Corner, into the stretch, my front runner was looking gutsy as she put away a rival.

In deep stretch, she was caught by three horses. Northern Prancer, my second choice, had gotten up for first at 13-1. The photo for second was between Arch Dieses, my third horse, and another outsider. I had done everything right. Whatever the outcome, I would make a considerable profit on the race. But if the photo went against me, which I fully expected, given my bad karma of late, then I would fall considerably short of the amount needed to move into an apartment.

The old Kipling lines made lots of sense here. "If you can meet with Triumph and Disaster, and treat those two impostors just the same..."

A peculiar serenity came over me. For the first time in my horseplaying life, I had done something professional. The Gods had even sent Brenda to me, as a test of my mental fortitude. Whatever the outcome, I had proven something to myself.

The numbers went up. My exacta had come in. With the proceeds from the win bet plus the exacta, I was going to collect one thousand two hundred dollars. Tomorrow morning I would move into a new apartment, the next day get a car and that weekend spend time with my kids.

I considered sticking around the track to see if I might double my money. The temptation was there to withdraw just a hundred from my winnings and put it on the nose of a 10-1, for another potential thousand-dollar return. I repeated to myself, "Stick to your strategy." Wait for the next big race to come along. If you can't wait, you shouldn't bet on horses.

There were two long bus rides from Santa Anita back to Curtis' house. The first left me downtown, on Olive Street. The second one took me to South Central. Both routes passed through the homeless neighborhoods around the downtown area. I looked out upon the masses of winos, bag women and demented mutterers, and wondered how many of them were men and women who had been beaten down by the court system, strung up by lawyers, worn down by a paranoid spouse, jinxed by a kinky resume.

I got off at Century Boulevard, where I found a street vendor. I bought a bouquet of flowers for Curtis' wife. Years later, not far from this corner, would be the focal point of the L.A. riots.

The day's events had Curtis grinning from ear to ear, especially my encounter with Brenda. Later that evening, I phoned for the results of the sixth race. I was curious which contenders had beaten Ingenuous? Any of the eight other horses, it made no difference. Brenda would be sorry she had seen me.

I listened to the announcer.

"The winner of the sixth race was an outsider, Ingenuous. Thirty-two sixty to win, sixteen forty and eight twenty. Second was..."

Down But Not Out

One night, my two kids slipped out of town. When I woke up the next morning, they were living with their mother's sister in Chicago. I didn't find out about the move until a day later, when I went to pick them up for visitation and they weren't there.

My daughter, Danielle, was old enough to explain it to me. Sure, she knew I had battled for custody, and that I loved them both. But two years after the divorce, they would see me happily married to Sonia and their mother suddenly seemed like the victim she had claimed to be all along.

"We felt guilty that we wanted to live with you, when you were the one who got the divorce. So now we just feel better away from both of you," she said over the phone.

There was nothing I could do about it. I figured, as they grew up, they would begin to see my side of the story. You can't deprogram kids over the phone. You can't even do it in person.

To compound my depression, two hours before the call from Danielle, I had made the dumbest decision of my race track life. I had two contenders in the feature at Hollywood Park, one of them 8-1 and the other 3-1, and I had played the 3-1. As the 8-1 was crossing the wire five lengths ahead of the field, I was asking myself why I had bet the lower-odds horse. Intellectually, I knew that you just don't split hairs when deciding between two contenders. You're supposed to bet the one with the highest potential payoff, you pinhead, or at least bet them both if the odds are high enough.

I had gotten home that evening just after Sonia had arrived from her bank job. Sonia and I had been married for a year. While she was cooking one of my favorite dishes, ginger chicken, Danielle had called.

When dinner was ready, I took my first and last bite. It was the best ginger chicken I had ever tasted, yet it made me nauseous. I had lost my kids and flubbed an important bet, one that could have turned my losing streak around.

"I'm sorry Sonia," I apologized. "Maybe I'll feel better later."

I explained about the 3-1 and the 8-1 and how you're supposed to bet the one with the higher odds. For the first time since I met her, her big, dark eyes welled up with outrage. Maybe I should have faked it and ate the chicken, but my rejecting her food was not the cause of her distress.

"I'm not sure I know you," she said. "Your children have just left you and you lose your appetite over a horse."

It was hard to fathom how a woman with such a soft voice could speak with such steely conviction.

"I have zero control over my kid's brainwashing but I should be able to follow simple betting rules at the track. I'm not sick over a horse, I'm pissed off at myself!"

"I've known you for three years, Matt, and you've never allowed a horse race to get the best of you."

"I've never had a losing streak like the one I'm in."

I wondered if my appetite would ever return. Maybe I'd need to be fed intravenously.

It's bad enough to go through a deep slump but the pain sharpens when you go over your betting records to try and decipher the cause of the collapse. Most players forget their losses pretty easily because they don't keep records. Or maybe it's the other way around. They don't keep records so they'll forget their losses. But for me, becoming a pro was part of my identity. I had to meet up with my ledger every night.

For the rest of the evening, Sonia was remote, perched in a corner of the living room, her fiery, rebuking eyes telling me that my obsession had spoiled the dinner she had prepared.

I could not find the words that would explain to a non-horseplayer the great difference between an obsession with betting and an obsession with becoming a pro. For several years I had been building a winning process, and now it was all eroding. That night at The Money Tree, I'd prescribed myself a little blues therapy. After the first set, I was seated at a table over my customary glass of red wine, when Curtis, the bass player, leaned toward me. I saw strands of grey hair in his goatee.

"Hey man," he said, "what's with you? You playin' tonight like a cocktail pianist."

Curtis was a man of few well-chosen words. "Cocktail pianist" meant that I had abandoned my customary dissonance. Dissonance is the muscle of jazz music. But it's risky to use dissonant chords. If they're not worked in with finesse, they come out sounding like flubbed notes. Curtis was right. Unconsciously, I had been playing too cautiously.

"No wonder I bet the 3-1 horse instead of the 8-1," I said to Curtis.

Emotionally wounded by my slump, my betting ego had become too timid. I had gone with the crowd rather than against it. You need discordant handicapping to beat the races.

The next day was no better. Richard Morella had a first-time starter going. No trainer in the United States was better at getting them ready to pop the first time. Articles had been written about this Morella specialty.

It was the four-horse in the second race. He had the typical Morella pattern, a seven-furlong workout to prepare for a six-furlong race. I bet the colt at 9-2. He finished third. That made five consecutive beaten first-timers from the Morella stable. His losing streak and mine seemed to coincide.

I was so taken aback by the parallel that I woke before

dawn the next day and drove down to Hollywood Park. I parked the Corolla in the dirt parking lot used by backstretch workers. I walked through the stable area, avoiding mud puddles as I went.

I spotted Morella in the cafeteria. Backstretch cafeterias are one of the last places in America where you can still find a true greasy-spoon breakfast. There was no heating in the place. The cold morning mist seeped into my bones. I filled a styrofoam cup with steaming coffee and went over to Morella's table.

"Excuse me, Mr. Morella," I said. "I've been a fan of yours for a long time. Richie Green's a friend of mine. He's one of your owners. Does that rate me a chance to ask you a question?"

"Well, why not?"

"How come suddenly you've been winning with second-time starters when it used to be you'd pop 'em first time out?"

"You're not packing a microphone, are you?" He looked me over.

"You can search me if you want."

"No, that's ok. Fact is that all them articles about me with first-time starters were hurtin' my business. You can't get too predictable in this game. Every now and then you've got to change.

That was all he had to say. Part of my losing streak had been caused by getting too hung up on continuity rather than change. The Morella bet was but one of these tired repetitions.

With each betting pattern, a handicapper has to decide whether several losses are a normal part of a down cycle with an inevitable upturn down the road, or whether that particular pattern is no longer valid.

In the midst of a losing streak, deciding what to do isn't easy. If you decide that a method is no longer valid and get off, you might discover the next day that it selected a $76.00

winner. On the other hand, remaining faithful to a flawed method in a changing racing game is also disastrous.

Later that afternoon, I met Sonia for lunch in Chinatown. I asked her for her opinion. Was I pressing? Mischievously she suggested we consult a fortune cookie. After cracking open my cookie, both of us could have been recruited by the New Agers. The message said: *The wise farmer plants more than one crop.*

"What do ya think the odds are against my getting this particular message?" I asked.

"It's just a coincidence," Sonia teased.

Some coincidence! The next afternoon, I drove to Hollywood Park with a fresh attitude. Curtis had shown me I had been playing it too safe. Morella had proven that the more one-dimensional handicapping angles are the most prone to radical change. The fortune cookie suggested that I should look at this thing with a more diverse perspective.

I went through the Hollywood Park turnstyle fully expecting my losing streak to turn around. Three hours later, I pushed the same turnstyle the other way without having cashed a ticket all afternoon. Hours of anguish awaited, battling the traffic on La Brea, passing dinner through a spasmic esophagus, painfully entering my losing bets in the unforgiving ledger, then trying to get my fingers to do it on the keyboard, to put some sort of spirit into My One And Only Love with no help from my brain or my soul. The folks who came to eat their charbroiled steaks and listen to music would be tolerant if I went through the motions. But Curtis and James would be on my case. I wanted to call in sick. But a bass-drum duo is no good without a piano.

At dinner, I thought I was maintaining an unbeat facade, but Sonia winced.

"If you're not hungry, I won't be offended. You lost again, didn't you?"

She didn't want to hear about the first-third in a potential $369 exacta or the lost photo in the maiden claiming race.

"I'm okay," I said.

"You're not okay. You're worried about the horses while millions of refugees around the world are sitting in tents, starving."

Wallowing in sorrow over my losing streak sounded pretty selfish, with all the real suffering going on. But precisely because of the rotten injustices, which I took all too seriously, the race track was my only refuge. Even in the music world, unfairness was the rule, with the odds tilted to favor a few. But at the track, every player, rich or poor, weak or powerful, played against the exact same odds.

Never mind that at the race track, each player is trying to remove the money from the other's wallet. Unlike any other venue in the world, race track competition is civil. Enemies share the same table, ask each other "who do ya like?".

The race track's fairness comes from the fact that those who win consistently do so because they put in the effort. Being from the right family or having gone to Harvard is of no advantage.

But racing for me was more than a refuge. It was the only activity I knew that helped me deal with death. Ever since my teenage years, death was on my mind. It was not fear, just a commitment that I was not going to allow my life to be soured by the downhill spiral of age.

With or without Sonia, I figured I'd still be betting horses from my death bed. For the worst case scenario, I even planned on how I could get in my action from a respirator. A friend would narrate the past performances. With no voice, I'd signal him with winks of the eye. Two winks, would mean the two-horse. Or if the eyes were failing, I'd signal with the fingers. A slight lift of the left pinky would be number one and so on. The bankroll would be on the night table.

Once my friend was off to the track with my bet, I would have something to hope for, a new surprise each day. No tomorrow was going to be the same as yesterday. I would never fade into a vegetative state, as long as the race track allowed me one more chance to find a new angle.

"Can't you see," I said to Sonia. "The race track is one of the things that keeps me alive."

"All I know," she responded, "is that if you take this too seriously now, you'll die young."

Sonia had a point. I needed to distance myself from the game, but without distancing myself from the horseplayer within. I was like a guerrilla band, needing a retreat to the hills for replenishment and redefinition.

The fortune cookie said I should cultivate diversity. To me that meant change the way I structured my whole life. My horseplayer self didn't leave me when I walked out of the track, so every routine in my life needed to be remolded.

I decided to get up early in the morning, even after my late night gigs. I'd run some laps through the neighborhood, like a repenting sinner. If necessary, I could take catnaps during the day. I would also take a break from the track, do some serious research and study my past records, as well as past performances and results charts.

I wouldn't stay home any more. I wasn't a fan of housing. A house was a necessity, a camp, a place to bed down, not the germination ground of new ideas. I needed to be out in the world. I'd drive Sonia to work downtown, leaving the Corolla in the parking garage of her bank. Then I would choose a public place as my "office." Pershing Square was out; drunks would see my racing forms and ask me for the winning double. The immense cafeteria beneath Sonia's bank building was extremely comfortable and could be an occasional haunt, but it had no windows. The walled-in feeling was not good for open-ended research.

I settled on the courthouse at the top of Hill Street. Symbolically, it made sense to be in a place of judgment. Back in my pre-Money Tree days, I had gone to the courts and hustled up Spanish interpreting jobs. I had learned to feel comfortable in that massive, stone structure.

The top floor cafeteria had picture windows on two sides. The back corner always had empty tables. There was a view spanning across the Harbor Freeway to a raunchy, meandering stretch of Sunset Boulevard, with Chavez Ravine in the background. Midmornings and after-lunch hours, the cafeteria was all mine.

Choice of place was no small decision. It was suddenly clear to me that everything you do outside the track has an impact on your wagering. In the morning you swat at a fly and in the afternoon you decide against using the three horse in your exacta, and somehow these two events have a secret connection.

By afternoons, with the lunch crowd thinning out, I'd be in my corner catnapping. The more often I dozed off, the better, for new ideas have a way of slipping into the head during transition periods between sleep and wakefulness. I figured that by 4:00 p.m., I'd have accomplished a day's labor. The last hour would be spent outside the bank building, taking in the sun, waiting for Sonia. I'd practice my waiting until it was crafted into an art. Waiting for a good bet is the horseplayer's highest art form.

Patience, I quickly learned, is also a researcher's ally. During the first day at Hill Street, studying the past performances and results charts unfortunately led to no meaningful discovery. Three hours went by. Shifting gears, I refilled my coffee and spread out my personal betting records. It was time to handicap the handicapper.

Pouring through my own records, some valuable evidence materialized. I keep a "book of why" in which each bet on the ledger is accompanied by a complete explanation of each betting decision. Going back through my winning periods as well as the latest crash, I learned that my most inspired betting decisions had been achieved while I was standing at the rail or walking around under the grandstand. Literally, I had been thinking better on my feet.

Both of this year's IRS payoffs had been the result of exacta inclusions made while walking from one haunt to another. A third big score had been fashioned while standing at the urinal. Meanwhile, none of my best decisions had come while seated.

This small discovery led to a greater one. During the prolonged losing streak, no more than twenty percent of my failures could be blamed on poor handicapping or methods gone awry. On the contrary, my handicapping had been more than adequate.

Without a doubt, the best book on betting horses is the player's own records. No expert's book would have explained that, for me, the difference between a winning and a losing streak was primarily one of decision making. And decision making was linked to things like attitude and inspiration.

I thought back to Curtis' critique of my unwillingness to take risks on the keyboard. I was in the same funk at the track. The bad streak was partly characterized by the fear of using my more outlandish handicapping discoveries. Part of that failure had to do with sit-down decisions but the other part was related to a backing-down attitude.

These patterns emerged from taking a break and studying my records. Had I now been playing on a daily basis, I never would have had the time to reflect on those records. Absence not only makes the heart grow fonder but the mind clearer.

My daily courthouse routine proceeded with orderly disorder. It was hard work poring through all those results charts, isolating all the first-time starters and layoff horses, then entering the records of each individual trainer for these vital specialties.

There were times when I wanted to take a coffee break. But a coffee break means going to a cafeteria and having a cup of coffee, and I was already in the cafeteria, with a cup of coffee in front of me all day. A true break meant going somewhere else.

I'd gotten to know the busboys very well. I was the only one who left tips for them. In exchange, they watched my results charts while I went on my break. For my break I decided to go down to say hello to Ernie, a bailiff and fellow horseplayer who helped process the landlord-tenant disputes on the seventh floor.

From my interpreting days there, I had learned all about the judicial ins and outs. Judge Erickson in Division Three, for example, would inevitably rule against the tenant and order an eviction, while Judge Phillips, in Division Fourteen, took the side of the underdog.

Whenever the Presiding Judge, a grumpy but fair oldtimer named Burns, assigned cases to the different divisions, the well-paid attorneys for the landlord would always use their option and ask for another judge if they were assigned to Division Fourteen, hoping they'd get Erickson.

Alternatively, those few tenants savvy or wealthy enough to come with a lawyer would ask for a different judge if they got stuck with Erickson in Division Three, hoping they'd draw Phillips.

When I arrived, Ernie was at the courtroom door, in his beige marshall's uniform. He was seeing to it that Judge Burns' court calendar rolled by as fast as possible, signing in the people scheduled to be heard.

"Matt, I thought you'd disappeared," he said, delighted to see me again. "Where've you been? Where's your Racing Form?"

I explained my plight. Ernie listened as he signed in the arrivals. His uniform and gun were the only signs that he was a cop. His velvety voice made nervous newcomers feel more at ease. He was a gentleman, with a stress on the gentle. He was from the only black family in a high desert town near San Bernardino. Like many desert people I knew, he was laid back and took things as they came. When he heard about my losing streak, he assured me that time would solve the problem all by itself.

"I know you're not here to work," he said, "but there's a young lady in there who needs help. Her name's Maria Gonzalez. You might want to give her a hand. She's nervous as all get out."

I never could tell whether Ernie tried to help these folks because he identified with them or simply because he was making Judge Burns' court calendar flow smoothly.

In a jittery Spanish with a Salvadoran accent, Maria Gonzalez explained to me that she had fallen behind in her rent after having had to pay hospital bills for her two-year-old son. The kid had gotten burnt by a faulty electric circuit in her apartment.

She showed me her documents, asked me if she had a chance to win. I looked at her past performances, discovering that she was a single mother who worked as a cleaning lady. I also saw that the notary whom she had paid to write out her response had failed to highlight her extenuating circumstances. Nevertheless, I couldn't make an odds line on her chances until she was assigned to a judge.

Burns came in. Ernie called the court to order and Burns said, typically, "alright, alright, let's get this calendar moving." As usual, he was impatient with people who did not respond promptly, the ones who were in a courtroom for the first time in their lives and felt intimidated by the new setting.

"Case number eleven, Shaeffer vs. Gonzalez."

"Attorney Whitehurst here, Your Honor, representing the plaintiff."

I knew Whitehurst from my previous stint in the courts. He had the look of a GQ model, suave, salon-tanned, nice guy in the hall, ruthless in the courtroom. L.A.'s worst slumlords depended on him. Maria's odds went a few ticks in the wrong direction.

"Come on, come on, where's the respondant?" Judge Burns said. "Come on, we don't have all day."

"Stand up, Maria," I whispered. "Just say your name."

"Maria Gonzalez."

Judge Burns looked down at his papers.

"Let's see, we'll send Schaeffer vs. Gonzalez to Division Three. Will plaintiff and respondant please come up and sign."

I had to make a quick decision. In Judge Erickson's Division Three, the favorite always won. Maria would be off the board. I whispered in Spanish.

"Division Three always rules against the tenant. Go up there and before you sign, ask for a different judge."

I watched her talking to the court secretary, then saw the secretary stand up and whisper to the judge.

Judge Burns sent out his next case, then announced: "I'm sending Schaeffer vs. Gonzalez to Judge Phillips in Division Fourteen."

"Your Honor," Whitehurst objected self-righteously. "The respondant obviously had no idea about the option. I see the interpreter back there." He pointed to me, as if his finger were the gun that upheld law and order.

"The interpreter was coaching her," he argued. "That's tantamount to practicing law without a license. I request this case be returned to Division Three. And I strongly recommend that this court take action against the interpreter."

There was nowhere to hide. Blood rushed up into my face. I had improvised and it looked like I'd played a bad chord. I had seen Whitehurst in action before. I wished I could confront him at the track, where we'd both get the same odds.

"Mr. Whitehurst," Judge Burns said. "The interpreter helps this calendar flow and you're disrupting the flow. Are you asking me to suspend Miss Gonzalez' constitutional right to her option?

Judge Burns must have remembered my little favors, the times he had said: "Mr. Interpreter, we have a respondant who can't afford an interpreter. Come on up here, you do it pro bono."

It was a fair exchange; Burns let me hang out in his court and I did an occasional pro bono job to help his calendar flow.

Now, the old man had come through. As Maria headed down the aisle, I gave her the high sign. She would be safe in Judge Phillips' Division Fourteen, where it was odds on that she'd escape the eviction. Had she been assigned to Judge Erickson, her best odds would have been 99-1 against her.

On my way out, Ernie patted me on the shoulder.

"Matt, don't be a stranger."

Back at my "office," my work fell into place. I had made a risky but correct decision with Maria Gonzalez. In appearance, the incident had nothing to do with my losing streak. But I knew otherwise. Success at the races is a holistic enterprise. If a person can handle making off-track decisions under stress, then he is ready to handle the races. The courtroom incident had been like a transfusion. Positive blood flowed through my veins for the first time in weeks.

Over the next three days, I discovered a number of trainer specialty bets to replace the Richard Morella first-time-starter angle. Although each trainer sample was small, to delay my betting until larger samples materialized would have been like waiting for Godot. Collectively the trainer specialties formed a little "mutuel" fund. If one of them fell apart, I would not get killed. I would not depend on one guy like Morella. This trainer mutuel fund would replace the 20 percent of my methods that needed to be scrapped.

The other 80 percent were still functioning. My losing streak in those categories was mainly due to a string of bad decisions. It was here that I made my most striking discovery. I had been betting my methods in a vacuum, without regard for the types of races in which they occurred. My visit to the tenant-landlord courts had triggered the discovery. Certain races gave the favorites a great advantage, equivalent to Judge Erickson's Division Three. But in other races, as with Judge Phillips' Division Fourteen, the favorite-longshot dynamic was reversed. My betting decisions had been taking place out of this vital context.

It wasn't simply a matter of taking risks, as Curtis had encouraged me to do. The risk had to be taken in the context of the "Division" where the favorites were false.

Armed with this new perspective, it was time to return to the track. Picking up a copy of the Form I discovered that the next day at Hollywood Park, I had two possible prime bets: a maiden dropper in the sixth and a Van Berg horse switching to Eddie Delahoussaye in the feature. I reminded myself that should both horses lose, I would be back again tomorrow with the same level of confidence.

Both the maiden claimer and the Van Berg stakes horse ran good races. The maiden finished third in a three-horse photo at 7-1 and the Van Berg horse got caught in traffic just when he was making his move into the stretch. By the time he had passed by my perch at the rail in mid-stretch, he was only beginning to find a hole. He made a belated charge and finished third. Good bets, bad result.

As planned, I had been on my feet for most of the time, so I was tired. It was an easy stroll from my spot at the rail to the exit at the beginning of the stretch. On my way out, I considered the ninth and last race. It was a mid-level claimer for colts and geldings, 4-years old and up, in which all of the entrants had recently lost at the same or lower class level. I call that a lesser-of-evils race.

It was not my intention to stay. I approached the turnstiles, stepping over tout sheets that had nailed both winners of the daily double. They had been printed up after the double was over, then strewn around the track as publicity.

As I waited for the line to thin out, I remembered something Curtis had said. At the club he had reminded me that dissonance was the name of the game. He had also contended that I was playing too cautiously, influenced by the doubt and vacillation that comes with a losing streak.

Suddenly it dawned on me that the ninth race was the equivalent of Judge Phillips' Division Fourteen. Conventional favorites could be virtually eliminated! It was a race that gave an edge to discordant longshots.

I walked back into the shadows of the immense grandstand, watching the toteboard along the way.

I felt as if I had just gotten out of Division Three and was now in the more favorable Division Fourteen. Suddenly, huge longshots had a good chance to defy their odds. False favorites set the stage for a feasible investment. To bet against them made sense, without even knowing what to bet *for*.

Straight No Chaser looked intriguing. The five-year-old gelding had lost six straight, but was reclaimed by Bill Spawr in his last race. If you dug back into the past performances, you could see that the horse had won twice for Spawr at high odds before being claimed away.

There was no action on Straight No Chaser but I left him in as a contender. On the other hand, the three-horse, Vin Rouge, had opened at 7-2 off a 12-1 morning line. Vin Rouge's odds were drifting up, suggesting that the early insider action was now being averaged in with the crowd's non-action.

Then there was Motel Swinger. Dead on the board at 20-1 throughout, with nine minutes to post, he went down to 11-1 in one flash. If that action was of the insider variety, he would be drifting up as the big bet got averaged in with the public's indifference. And so he did.

I'm not a believer in conspiracies. Often, stables like their own horse but don't consider the others. Their action is meaningless. But when the others all stink, suddenly the stable action becomes significant.

Five minutes before post, Vin Rouge was up to 6-1, Straight No Chaser was at 18-1 and Motel Swinger was back to 20. I bet ten bucks to win on the two horses with the highest odds, then keyed the Spawr reclaim, Straight No Chaser, back and forth with the two others. I threw in a one-dollar trifecta box of the three. My total investment was $34.

They began the six furlongs on the backstretch. Vin Rouge stalked close to the two leaders. Motel Swinger was running in fourth place. I couldn't see Straight No Chaser. No doubt he was near the back of the pack.

Into the turn, Vin Rouge picked up his pace, catching the tiring leaders by the time they hit the stretch. From the rail near the turn, I had a good view of Vin Rouge. He was being hand ridden. His stride was long and easy. He looked like the winner.

My pulse leaped out of control. If Vin Rouge won without one of my place horses, I was not covered. Motel Swinger emerged from a cluster of horses to move into second place. If he won, I'd collect at 20-1, but I doubted he'd catch Vin Rouge.

Suddenly, I understood why the Aztecs found volunteers for human sacrifice. Even though two of my horses were going to be one-two in the exacta, I was not covered unless Straight No Chaser made it into the trifecta. Passing my spot on the rail, Straight No Chaser was moving through a cluster of horses. The ones in front of him were shortening stride.

As they crossed the wire, I could only see them from behind. Vin Rouge was called the winner by a half length. Motel Swinger was second. The one I needed was in a photo for third.

I tried to ignore my inner convulsions as the red photo sign glowed on the board.

Dumb decision in not boxing all three horses in the exacta. So what if a three-horse exacta box is the wrong strategy in the long run. I had the short run to consider. I would go off with the Trappist Monks, or join one of those long pilgrimages in South America where by the time you get to the cross on top of the mountain, your feet are bloodied and your clothes in tatters. I would volunteer for the Iron Maiden. I wanted to feel the nails dig into me, slowly piercing as the Maiden closed in at one millimeter per second.

The photo sign went off. The six went up. It was Straight No Chaser. There was no roar. Few players had it. It was an I.R.S. job. The tri paid two thousand six hundred and I had half of it.

I had gone to the courthouse on Hill Street to research the race charts. But tracing the hidden connection of this bet, it came back to the courts themselves. Had it been a Division Three race, Judge Erickson would have determined the outcome. But the ninth race at Hollywood Park fit the description of Division Fourteen. The favorite had little chance. It was the right scenario to go for a price.

In one race, my bad streak had been neutralized. Tomorrow, I would be starting from scratch. Sooner or later, the research I had done at Hill Street was going to pay off. In the meantime, I had to be prepared to bet on races where my improvising skills and the dissonance I loved so much could play a role.

On the way up La Brea, I stopped off at a 7-11 and called Sonia. I wanted to intercept her before she began cooking.

"Let's go out to eat."

I wanted to celebrate.

"I've already got some ginger chicken going," she said. "Why don't you pick up a nice bottle of wine instead."

I would eat a good dinner. There was no need to tell Sonia what had happened at Hollywood Park, that my losing streak was over. She would see me serving myself again and again and she would know.

THE ELIMINATOR

It was one of those rare days when my whole philosophy of life boiled down to one horse. Monk's Corner was going to raise us a notch in the tax brackets. He was going to pay for a balcony flat on the Mediterranean, overlooking topless sunbathers.

It was one of those days when I knew something that no one else in the crowd knew. Monk's Corner was entering the third race after having run several bad ones. He was dropping in class and switching to Eddie Delahoussaye. Buried deep in his past performances, prior to the ten races listed in the Form, were two matching situations when he had switched to Eddie D. and won at a big price.

I was going to make the largest bet of my career. I was going to play Monk's Corner to win and box him in exactas with everything that could walk. I leaned over the fence of the Santa Anita paddock, surrounded by flowers, bathed in mellow sun, caressed by a sweet breeze. This was my day.

The horses strolled into the circular walking ring, riders at their sides. For one moment, I was Degas, capturing the sensorial flow of these shiny animals, along with the pastels of the riders' silks. And there he was, Monk's Corner, number 7. At his side, Delahoussaye wore turquoise, adding to the splendor.

Two men in jeans stood to my left, making observations in Spanish. From their demeanor I identified them as backstretch employees. One of them said:

"El siete no tiene posibilidad."

What does he mean, the seven has no chance?

"The seven's gonna win," I interrupted.

The guy who had eliminated Monk's Corner switched to English.

"The seven has no chance."

"What makes you say that?" I asked, desperately.

"His walk. His tail. A few other things."

"I'm gonna bet that horse," I said, defiantly.

"You're gonna lose."

The jockeys mounted their horses and the two grooms went up through the grandstand to observe the post parade. I followed them. After the horses pranced by, I asked the opinionated one what gave him the right to eliminate horses on the basis of appearances.

"I grew up with them." He pointed. "Look at the seven. He got a tentative stride, as if he were trying to avoid hitting the ground. I say he's lame."

I was not about to change my bet because of some groom's opinion. In Spanish, the companion said:

"Rene nunca falla"("He's never wrong.")

"Then who's gonna win," I asked.

"That I can't say," Rene answered. "I can tell you the ones that are not going to win but I can't predict the winner."

To me, that sounded like a painfully honest answer, unburdened by ego, as if Rene were for real.

I fingered the wad of bills I had planned to bet and drew out a twenty from my right pocket, one tenth of my original investment. If Monk's Corner won at 12-1, I'd be kicking myself for sure, but I was just going to put in twenty to win.

I went back up to the M section of the grandstand, with Al and Larry. Monk's Corner broke well and was pressing the leaders from outside. He was in perfect position. On the turn, he began to accelerate. As he passed the leaders three wide, my whole body writhed in a spasm of self-hatred. Why had fate placed me next to that strange groom? Why had I listened to him? The seven was going to sweep by the field and I was going to miss the greatest score of my race track life.

As they hit the stretch, Monk's Corner seemed to run up against an invisible wall. He began to back up. By the time they had passed mid stretch, below our perch, Monk's Corner was huffing and puffing in last place.

I told Al and Larry what had happened. Thanks to Rene, I had saved $180.

I went back down to the paddock and waited for Rene and his friend. In the next race, Rene picked out three horses that were not going to win. One of them was the favorite.

He was right again. All three were out of the money. I rounded up all my race track cronies and proposed a deal. If each of us offered Rene five bucks a day, we might have ourselves a consultant. By readily eliminating horses, we would overcome the "take" and have a mathematical edge. Even random betting would be profitable once we could toss out at least 30 percent of the betting pool.

I went back down to the paddock and proposed the idea. Rene was ready and willing. But on days when his stable had a horse running, he would not be available. It was the small stable of Cesar Vallejo, so we'd have his services most of the time.

As I began to hang out with Rene, I learned that he was in the States illegally. He had been a heavy drinker back in El Salvador and one hot afternoon, he had come out of a bar after having cleaned off a whole shelf of beers. A procession of striking teachers was chanting, down with this and up with that. Relishing the excitement, Rene groped for words, randomly. He shouted, "Long live the strikers," just when the government troops were descending on the march.

Rene was arrested as an agitator for the teachers' strike. At police headquarters, he explained that he had dropped out of school after the third grade, so how could he be an agitator?

"Let me go and I promise I'll lay off the liquor."

His defense made no impact on the stone-faced men in uniform. He was locked up for six months.

When he got out, he made his way north, swimming across two rivers, through Guatemala and into Mexico. He arrived in Mexico during a presidential election campaign. Chanting Mexican slang like a virtuoso, he talked his way into a job with the dominant party. His job got him standing in the back of a slow-moving pick-up truck, where he shouted "Long Live Portillo," and gave political speeches consisting of a script of stale cliches. He voted five times in the election.

When the election was over, his source of income vanished, he walked over an old railroad bridge into Laredo, Texas. He had been working at odd jobs here and there, from Chicago to L.A., mainly in kitchens and on farms picking fruit and vegetables.

He was now tired, he said, doing jobs that no one else wanted. A civil war was raging in his country but he was thinking of returning anyway.

"If we all left the U.S. at once," he said, "your restaurants would go bankrupt and produce prices would hit the sky."

"What about your lady?" I asked. "You gonna dump her?"

Rene was living with a woman three times his size. His taste in women was eclectic. Physical traits made absolutely no difference. He had gone from a tall, bony woman to a burly fat one. So long as they were kind and gentle.

"Maritza understands. She says that if she didn't have a daughter, she might go with me. Besides, there's another lady. My mother. I wanna see my mother."

As days went by, he became more defiant. On his off day, he went to eat lunch at the Department of Immigration cafeteria, as if to say, "Here I am, deport me."

One day, Rene told us that he had quit his job. He was going to return to El Salvador. I told him we'd double his salary and got the guys to raise our individual contributions to ten bucks a day. Occasionally, a horse that Rene had eliminated would win a race. But only occasionally. And where it really counted, with favorites, Rene had only been wrong once.

The next Sunday morning, the phone rang. It was Rene, saying he was sorry, but he was leaving for El Salvador in the morning.

"Give us two days," I pleaded, "and teach us how you do it. We'll pay you tuition."

"I'm not sure I can explain it. I grew up with horses. It's something I can feel."

I believed him. If I hadn't grown up hearing Thelonius Monk and Herbie Hancock, I doubt that even the best of music classes would have taught me how to improvise on the keyboard.

Rene agreed to spend all Sunday afternoon at the track and take a stab at explaining how to understand the horses' body language. In exchange for the favor, he asked me to take him to the airport Monday. He had a one-way ticket to El Salvador.

The lesson did me no good. I was never going to catch on. I made one last attempt to convince him to stay, even offered him a free room at our house. But his decision was final.

I accompanied him to the gate at LAX.

"What if you have to fight in the war?" I asked. "Which side will you choose?"

"Whichever offers me a better life."

The lady behind the counter at the boarding gate examined Rene's ticket.

"I'll need to see an I.D. from El Salvador."

"I don't have any I.D.," Rene said.

"Anything will do, a birth certificate, passport..."

"I have none."

"Then you can't board."

"Look," he said. "I can sing the Salvadoran national anthem. No one else knows that song."

He began to sing.

"I'm sorry," she cut him off, "but we're required to see identification. They won't allow you into El Salvador if you don't have I.D. Take this voucher. You can pick up your refund at the ticket counter."

I argued with the lady, to no avail. On the way out, I suggested that he stick it out in the U.S.A. Rene insisted that I take him to the Greyhound Station. He would ride to Tijuana. From there he would talk his way through Mexico. He still had his Party I.D., and he knew all the Mexican slang words. In Mexico City, he'd get the Salvadoran embassy to give him safe passage through Guatemala, where another war was raging.

On Wednesday, I returned to Santa Anita. Standing at the paddock, I marveled at my ignorance. I was investing money on live animals on the basis of numbers on a piece of paper. I was reading the music without having grown up with it.

As the horses strode into the walking ring prior to the first race, I wondered whether I should be playing against such a disadvantage. Maybe I should quit and drift into something more predictable.

But then I thought of Rene. He represented the majority of the human race, confronting a life-and-death struggle in an irrational world. By comparison, the race track, with all its uncertainties, was a mellow refuge. I admired the creatures that paraded before me. No doubt several of them would have been eliminated by Rene. But they were all here to carry on with the spectacle.

THE RELUCTANT TOUT

I had just left a bet on the feature at Hollywood Park. I made my way through the late-afternoon Pavillion crowd to the escalator. My goal was to beat the rush hour traffic, but the real traffic was right where I was. I had run into a one-man blockade.

He was big and flabby. Whoever manufactured him had screwed on a head a few sizes too large for his body..

"Excuse me," he said. "You must be Matt. Can I talk to you for a moment?"

His deep and full voice didn't fit with his boyish face.

"I'm on my way out," I said. "Walk me down the escalator."

"Jack told me about you."

"Who's Jack?" I asked.

"You know, your mutuel clerk."

I kept to one clerk, occasionally tipping him. That way, if I was ever at the end of a line and in danger of getting shut out, I'd be able to get in my bet instantaneously.

"Jack says you win. I need a tout."

His wobble was straightened out by the descending escalator. I was two steps below him. He was imposing from my vantage point, especially that big head of his.

"How do you know Jack's not jivin' you?" I asked.

"It's my job to know people. He says you're all business. Says you collect on big fucking longshots."

"So why would I need to be a tout," I asked.

I could have answered my own question. I was not putting enough money through the windows, passing too many races and rarely crushing the ones I hit.

"We all can use money, can't we?" he grinned.

Off the escalator and out into the glaring afternoon sun, I said:

"Look." I held up my Form. "You've got all the touts you need, right here."

There were ads for 900 numbers, monthly and whole-meet rates, seminars.

"I've tried all those jerkoffs. They can't pick an apple off a tree."

I knew most of the L.A. touts. A few were corrupt hustlers but most were reputable. But they didn't tell their public that they were at a serious disadvantage picking horses in the morning, before knowing the odds. I had once tried betting blindly myself, tried it with a bookie. You save time and overhead that way. I had started out with a few longshots, but after six months, I was at the break-even point and I quit. My style of play required the toteboard.

"Look, my name's Wilson Tripp. I believe in word of mouth. Touts that solicit can't be good. I found you, you didn't find me. I can make you a reasonable offer."

"I just don't see myself as a tout," I said.

"Come on, you gotta help me. I got backers, you see. They spotted me a twenty thousand dollar bankroll. It's down to ten. I'm in deep shit. Jack says you know what your doin'."

"Look, Wilson, here's my phone number. I wanna beat the traffic. Call me later. I'll think about it!"

When I arrived at our apartment on Burbank Boulevard, Sonia told me I had just missed a call. From someone named Wilson. He said he would call back within a half hour, to please not go anywhere until he called.

"Who's this Wilson? He sounds weird," Sonia said.

I told her about the tout offer, said that I was going to turn it down.

"You don't even know how much you'll get," she said. We were seated in the living room. With the windows open, you could hear the freeway traffic, like a grinding ocean. Neither of us had noticed the noise until after we'd rented the place.

"If my handicapping gets tied up in other peoples' fortunes, I'm likely to mess up," I explained. "I don't like being responsible for other people's money. The pressure distorts my reasoning."

"Matt," she said. "You have an offer to get paid for doing what you love the most. You handicap every day anyway. Why not take the bonus?"

Sonia was making more money than I was. With my child support payments, I was always on the edge of tap city. These were the things going through my mind when I said the wrong words.

"Looks like I'm obligated to take the gig. You're the real breadwinner in this house."

"Matt, I'm surprised at you. I thought you were beyond that kind of hangup. Never have I compared incomes. I thought you knew things like that are not important to me. From now on I'll keep my opinions to myself. Go do what you want."

Sonia was tough. But inside she was hurting. I had been foolish to think that she would hold it over me, I mean the fact that she earned more from her bank job than I did by playing the piano. One day she might make it to CEO and still, she would never think of keeping score. I hadn't intended to say such a dumb thing. It just came out that way.

I followed her to the kitchen. I tried to take her hand, but she shook it away.

"Look, baby, I'm sorry."

"Never once have I tried to make our life a contest," she said.

I took her hand. This time she let me hold it.

"Hey, look," I said. "Sometimes the pressure gets to me. You see how this Wilson Tripp is gonna be nothing but trouble."

"Matt, you should try my job just for one day to understand the meaning of pressure. If the offer is good, why not take the job and just keep handicapping like you always have. It's simple. Just don't let other people make an impact."

The phone rang. It was Wilson. Since he was soliciting me and not the other way around, he owed me an explanation. He explained that he was a commodities trader. He had bragged to his clients how the race track offered lucrative opportunities. He thought he was a good handicapper. But as soon as he had their twenty thousand, he began to lose. He had tried the seminars, the 900 numbers, to no avail.

"Look, Wilson," I can't give you picks without seeing the odds. I might tell you I like the 3-horse and then I get to the track and the 3's going off at 7-5 and I bet the 6-horse 'cause he's the overlay."

"No problem," he said. "You just tell me the odds you can take. On days you can't go, I can put in your action. But I hope we'll be able to spend some time together. I have a table there. I'll buy you lunch and I can pay you $200 a month, and put in a few free bets for you along the way."

"Well, let me think about it."

"How about another $200 if you can come up with two picks a day for my friend Hank in New York. Hank's a tout. He's having trouble finding good handicappers."

Four hundred a month would cover most of my child support. There was no extra labor for Hollywood Park. The New York part of the bargain sounded easy enough. I didn't have to handicap nine races in order to pick two. I'd just scan the New York past performances, pick out the two races that fit most with my specialties, and come up with two horses.

Sonia was right. I'd be getting paid for doing what I liked.

New York began well, or so I thought. But Hank saw it from another perspective. When I picked several losers in a row, Hank got desperate. His clients were going to lynch him, he explained, if I didn't improve my hit rate, if he didn't have a winner TODAY.

Hank was more like a client than a tout. He was just as desperate as Wilson. He let me know that his business depended on my picks.

Wilson too had clients, perhaps less forgiving ones than Hank had. Wilson's syndicate of clients were commodities players straddling the underworld. He had lured their money with his sales skill. The races were easy, he said. A favorite to show at $2.80 means 40 percent profit in one minute and eleven seconds. Forty percent is a big number for any investor. If that didn't persuade them, then the one minute and eleven seconds would.

Picking them without the benefit of seeing the odds was a risky enterprise. I consulted my venerable friend and occasional tout, Don Quick, who lived and bet up in Berkeley.

"If you gotta pick 'em in the morning," he advised, "go for price. That's the only way you come out with a profit."

Don Quick had the lowest hit rate of all the touts I knew, 22 percent, but he was the only one who produced a bottom line profit at the end of the meet. He was also the only one who issued monthly statements to his clients.

So with both Hank and Wilson, I went for price. My first week with Hank gave me one winner in ten picks, but that winner paid $31.20, so I had a 33 percent profit. Hank called:

"Hey Matt, what's this one-for-ten deal? Wilson told me you're good. I hope we can get better this week."

"Hank," I said. "I did better than the best mutual fund. We're talking about 33 percent profit!"

"What do my clients know about profit?" Hank said over the phone. "They want winners. Every day."

"You mean they'd rather collect more often but lose money?" I asked.

"This is my business. The clients who didn't call me the day you had the thirty-dollar winner were 0 for 8 last week. They'll quit on me, profit or no profit. And the other ones had less money on the 15-1 'cause he was a longshot. So YOU SAY it's a profit and I SAY it's a loss. I want winners. I don't care if the fuckers pay three sixty or thirty-six dollars."

If Hank hadn't been so dogmatic, I would have suggested some new ideas, like educating his clients to manage their money. But he was too cynical. And who knows, maybe he was right about his clients and I was wrong.

Alright, with Hank, I would have to simply look for winners and disregard price. That made my job easier. But with Wilson, I needed to get his bankroll moving in the right direction. The second morning on the job, Wilson called to ask if I was going out to the track. I had a commitment at the U.S.C. music school to work on some new arrangements with Curtis and James.

I gave Wilson one single horse. It was a Mandella turf horse in the seventh. I called the results line from U.S.C. to hear that my horse had come in and paid $22.00. Wilson had put ten on him for me, at no charge. It was a no lose proposition.

He phoned at dinner time. I looked forward to listening to a happy client.

"Hey, Wilson, we're on our way," I chirped.

"Matt, you better pack me in ice," he responded glumly.

"Whadayamean?"

"Don't worry, I bet him for YOU."

"And yourself?"

"I wheeled him and backwheeled him in the exacta."

That meant Wilson had played the horse on top and on bottom with every other horse in the field, thus assuring an exacta payoff, so long as the key horse won or placed. Only problem was that the favorite had finished second, making the exacta payoff so low that Wilson had only made a small profit on the race, about as much as if he had bet a favorite to show.

"Matt, if you're not there with me tomorrow, you might as well pack me in ice."

The Pavillion needed to hire an extra bartender and cook for Wilson. When he won, he ate. When he lost, he drank, usually straight-and-hard stuff.

During the week, my being there with Wilson was having no positive impact. In fact, I had dipped into a slump. But after each of my losers, Wilson would console me, then take out a wad of bills and bet an even money favorite to win, five hundred here, two hundred there. It was a self-destructive habit of his, trying to get it all back by pressing with favorites, but temporarily it was working. I was not in a position to tell him he was wrong; he was collecting while I was just giving him losers.

Compared to Hank, Wilson was a true sport. I had picked four of ten for Hank in my second week, none of them paying more than $5.60, two of them under even money. One morning, while Sonia and I were eating breakfast, Hank called. He sounded grimmer than ever.

"If I want all chalk, Matt, I can buy the consensus for a quarter."

"But I was doing what you..."

"I need winners, but I need 'em to pay enough to keep my callers happy."

Exasperated, I gave him a couple of longshots and hung up. I told Sonia what had happened.

"Call him back, Matt. You didn't make your case."

I dialed Hank's number. He heard my voice, and reacted defensively.

"I know, I know, Matt, I was pressuring you and now you're not sure about your longshots. But you know what'll happen? If you tell me not to use them, they'll win."

"Hank, that's not it. I've done everything you asked and you're still not happy. I'm quitting."

"Matt, what kinda shit is this?"

In frustration I hung up.

Sonia was drinking her watery coffee.

"Matt, I didn't say you should act just like him. Instead of making your case, you cut him off."

"Next time Hank calls, YOU talk to him. Then you'll understand. And I don't know how the hell you can drink that painted water."

One minute and thirty seconds later, Hank called back:

"Matt, now look, I'm sorry. You gotta understand. My clients drive me up the wall. They want a winner every time, and they want price too. Don't quit on me now."

"It's your fault, Hank. You boxed yourself in a corner with your own ads. You give them unrealistic expectations. Just advertise the truth."

"If I do that, I don't get nobody."

Hank's blame-it-on-Matt posture made Wilson seem like a saint. Hank had no right to gripe.

Wilson should have complained but didn't. I had given him a week of losers. "Don't worry, Matt, you're gonna pick a big one tomorrow," he'd say.

Meanwhile, Wilson continued to rescue himself from what would have been a serious losing streak by betting big on low-priced horses. In the short run, it was working. But in the long run, that strategy would kill him.

"Hey waiter, bring this man a scotch, no water, right Matt?" Wilson tried to console me.

"No scotch, Wilson, just orange juice," I said.

"Whadaya mean? Your horse just threw the jockey. You need something hard. Give the man a vodka and orange juice."

I was feeling guilty now, being wined and dined by a man who might end up dead in a dark alley if I didn't come up with winners.

It was here that I faced the classic dilemma. Do I modify my play and look for lower-priced horses, just to collect, or do I continue to go for a good price. I chose the latter. Had I been with anyone else, I could have become a presser. But Wilson encouraged me to be myself.

The next afternoon, with an actor/musician friend Nick at our table, I could only come up with one horse, a turf longshot by the name of Woodcote. Woodcote had legitimate excuses in his last five races. He had just lost one that was taken off the grass and put on dirt, probably remaining in the race to satisfy the racing secretary's need to keep the field large enough to be bettable.

On another occasion, Woodcote had been forced wide on the first turn, virtually eliminated, then had made a bold move only to die in the stretch. Still another time, he had been given a front-running trip in a pace duel when he should have laid back and stalked the pace. He had been through a series of races that had not allowed him to show his true ability.

"Matt, you better have the ambulance waiting for Woodcote."

"Look back to his legitimate races, Wilson. He's got a chance at a price."

"He's got Ortega. Ortega can't even ride a merry-go-round."

Ortega had finished second on the horse at 35-1 nine races back.

"Ortega's right for this horse, Wilson."

"Ippolito's a cold trainer. He thinks the winners' circle is an ancient mythical place."

"I don't know what to say, Wilson. He's got a square chance to win and he'll be at least 15-1."

"What do you think, Nick?" my client asked.

Nick was having a full-course lunch thanks to Wilson's generosity, so he felt obligated to give his opinion.

"Matt's got a point," Nick said, trying to swallow and talk at the same time. "I'm gonna bet him."

Wilson proceeded to lose three of four bets, collecting once at even money. Empty whiskey glasses accumulated on our table.

Woodcote opened in the betting at 10-1. By the time they were coming out on the track for the post parade, he was at fifteen.

"I can't do it, Matt. Mr. Ed would have a better chance here."

Woodcote had gone up to 30-1.

"At those odds, he's worth a bet, Wilson."

Nick and I went outside to watch the race, although from the rail, at the Pavillion, we would have a terrible head-on view when they came down the stretch.

"Don't you think you should be more assertive with Wilson?" Nick asked.

"Not with the string of losers I've had. I gave him the evidence on Woodcote and I defended the horse every step of the way. I just hope he bets him."

If Wilson had made a bet, it wouldn't have been at his usual $500 or else he would have impacted the tote odds. By the time they came to post, Woodcote was 45-1! No one had made a large bet on him.

Woodcote was off to a clean start, grabbing the rail before the first turn. For once, he had a little luck in his favor. On the first turn, the favorite went four wide, virtually eliminating himself.

On the backstretch, Woodcote was running mid-pack, just where you're supposed to be in a grass race, since the front runners usually fade in the stretch.

On the far turn, I lost sight of them, while the noise of the crowd muffled the PA announcer. Nick, whose keen eyes proxied for mine, said that Woodcote was waiting for room. As they hit the stretch, Nick narrated:

"The whole field is fanning wide. It's opening up for him. Woodcote's coming through on the rail."

He advanced from mid-pack to third. When they hit the wire, still head on, I couldn't tell if he'd gotten up or not. I had him twenty and twenty, so even if he placed, I'd still collect a sizeable payoff; the favorite, who would have drained the place price, was off the board.

"I'll take the place price," I said.

"You're talkin' like a defeatist," Nick said. "The fucker got up."

The photo light went off and Woodcote's number went up. I would be collecting over a thousand dollars. A small part of me, the part that takes on a moral responsibility for the fate of others, did not allow me to completely savor the victory. Nick and I were looking back towards the glass windows of the Pavillion to spot Wilson.

"Don't worry, Matt. If Wilson didn't have him, it's not your fault."

He had come out to look for us.

I yelled, "Tell me you had 'em, Wilson...Say that you had 'em."

Wilson shook my hand.

"I didn't have a penny on him. You better pack me in ice. Bury me in horse shit."

He held out a $200 win ticket. He had bet the favorite.

"Wilson, I don't understand," I said. "You bet five hundred sometimes, at even money. You only needed twenty on Woodcote to collect nine hundred. For you, twenty is pocket change."

I had been hard on myself for not betting more. Now I realized that lots of the guys who could really pull the trigger were machos at even-money and wimps at ten to one.

We had come in Nick's car. On the way home, Nick offered some friendly advice.

"Matt, you worry too much about the other guy. You don't even order a whole dinner with Wilson 'cause you're protecting his budget. He's a big boy now. There's only so much you can do."

"I could have told him, bet Woodcote or else."

"If you did that, you'd be a psychologist and not a tout. You'd have to charge him a thousand a month, and that would be cheap."

Nick made sense. During the next weeks, I went into a tailspin at Belmont, and my phone conversations with Hank were spoiling my breakfasts.

"Matt," Hank said, "you can't even pick your nose lately. My clients are gonna kill me, Give me a winner. Give me two."

"Hank, I've had it. I'm a longshot handicapper and I work for a long-term profit. If I try to work within your guidelines, it's not me anymore."

"You mean you're quitting on me."

"I got no choice."

He was probably glad to see me go. He offered no resistance.

"What horses were you gonna give me?" he asked.

"I had Blue And Black in the third and Lobotomy in the seventh."

The next morning, Hank called.

"Matt," he said. "Blue And Black won. He paid in double figures. So did Lobotomy."

"Did you use 'em?" I asked.

"Use 'em. What do ya mean use 'em. You quit on me, remember? I couldn't sleep last night, I was so sick. I couldn't even take it out on my wife. She was out of town. How about you give me another week of picks?"

Instead I gave him Nick's phone number, told him Nick was good. I knew that win or lose, Nick would not get wrapped up in Hank's ups and downs. So long as Hank paid on time, he'd get his picks.

When the horses moved to Del Mar, I called most of my picks in to Wilson over the phone. One Saturday, he invited Nick and me to meet him at Del Mar.

This time I drove us in the 1982 Honda Civic I had bought with the winnings from a trifecta. On the way down, as we were passing the San Onofre nuclear power plant, with the Pacific Ocean in the background, Nick explained how he was doing with his new tout job. Rather than study the races, he was having a friend in Las Vegas fax him Dave Litfin's handicapping column and was picking out the two best arguments each day. It took him five minutes. Hank could have done the same thing, for free. Nick was doing fine.

Wilson told us his backers were asking about their money and he didn't know what to tell them.

"I told them we were down a little and not to worry," Wilson said. "If they knew how bad it was, they might gun me down once and for all."

Now he was going to put in a Pick Six and hope for the big score that would erase the long nightmare. He was alive after two races of the Pick Six, but all four of his choices in the third leg lost.

Our table had a view of the rail near the finish line. Wilson was drinking whiskeys and leering at the women in bikinis and shorts.

"I'm just gonna look at big boobs all afternoon, then I'll drive to Tijuana and whore it up, and then I'll find a cliff and jump off into the sea. It's all over for me. Look at those knockers down there. I love Del Mar."

Nick and I had a horrendous afternoon. We left the track before the last race, each of us buying a ten-dollar exacta box. We could send in the tickets and collect by mail if we won.

Wilson had changed his mind about TeeJaying it. He convinced us to visit his home in Irvine. We met him there. We were introduced to his wife, a stately woman who hardly fit with Wilson.

"This is my lady, Harriet," he said. "She kicked me out of the house the night I told her I didn't have Woodcote. She said, how can you pay this man and then not use his advice?"

We had a drink, then got up to leave. Wilson came out from the kitchen.

"Gentlemen, I phoned the race results. You had the exacta."

Nick and I had recouped a large chunk of the money we had lost. Wilson made a suggestion.

"I can cash your tickets for you. I have to go down to Del Mar again tomorrow. If you want, I'll write you each a check for your winnings; you just give me your tickets."

Nick hesitated, but when he saw me hand Wilson my ticket, he did likewise. A few days later, we found out that Wilson's checks had bounced.

I phoned his home. Harriet told me she hadn't seen him since the Sunday of our visit.

A week later, I received a phone call from Wilson.

"Matt, I've been shacked up in this hotel with a beautiful blond. She just blew with the rest of my bankroll. I'm gonna have to lay low for a few months. Sorry about the bad checks."

"Wilson, where are you?"

"It makes no difference."

I waited a month, then tried to call him. His phone was disconnected.

"Do you think he packed himself in ice?" I asked Nick.

"Shit, if the fucker couldn't even put twenty on Woodcote, he sure as hell doesn't have the guts for that."

When the Hollywood Park winter meet began, Nick and I went to the Pavillion and looked for Wilson. We figured he'd be in the same dining room as always. He wasn't there.

The waiter didn't recognize the name Wilson, so we described him, the big head, the wobbly walk, and the waiter knew exactly who it was.

"I ain't seen him for a long time."

Each afternoon, we'd scour the Pavillion, the Clubhouse, the Grandstand. Not a sign of Wilson.

A few months later, I had a gig in D.C. I took advantage of

the opportunity to go to the Library of Congress, where they have computerized records of all listed phone numbers in the U.S.A. I checked every region of the country, under Wilson Tripp, and then under Tripp Wilson. I even looked under Harriet Tripp. There was nothing.

Although he might have had an unlisted number, my suicide hypothesis was a step nearer to becoming a legitimate theory. Nick insisted it couldn't be suicide.

"Wilson would have needed someone like Kevorkian to pull the plug. And I doubt Kevorkian accepts gambling losses as a legitimate reason for suicide."

That left two possibilities. Either he was living somewhere under an assumed name or his backers had done him in. We made a line. The first possibility was 4-5. The second was 6-5.

BUMPS AND GRINDS

Like me, Nick burned out on being Hank's tout and quit. Nick was a fifties rock 'n roller, a sixties veteran of the drug culture and a chain-smoking actor with a natural talent for playing the role of Cicero bad guys.

Although he was best on the old acoustic guitar, Nick had accepted the electric sound with no complaint. His stage uniform featured a Twenties dark suit vest over a Lenny Bruce T-shirt.

Even though it appeared that Nick had further adjusted to contemporary life by becoming a whiz at the computer, his true age seemed to have come and gone with the arrival of non-smoking flights and disco music.

Like his betting colleagues, Al, Dick, Gene and Mark, Nick was also an ex-New Yorker. I was the only Chicagoan of the group. Generally, Nick wasn't fond of hanging out with horseplayers. He thought they were mainly self-destructors. But his New York past brought him close to these men—the gambling with baseball cards, the stickball games that extended into dusk under dim street lights. They all knew how to parallel park into a space only 3 millimeters longer than their own car. They knew how to fish Spaldeen rubber balls out of deep sewers with twisted hangers.

They had all grown up in either Queens, Manhattan or Brooklyn, the last being Nick's turf. They had all experienced an authentic street life that is unheard of in modern suburbia or car-dominated L.A. Perhaps that's why Nick was living, with his second wife, in raunchy Hollywood, where all the goods and services needed for daily life are within a five-minute walk. It didn't seem accidental that Larry, Al, Gene and Nick were all horse playing actors, either. After all, they had grown up in a town where off-Broadway and Aqueduct were focal points of the action.

Nick, the old roller-hockey champ, still had lots of toughness built into his small frame. Getting checked into brick playground walls or dumped onto concrete will either make you or break you. In his mid-thirties, Nick appeared as if he could still skate onto the playground and hold his own against the toughs of Hollywood High.

His thick black hair, bushy eyebrows and piercing dark eyes just happened to coincide with a composite sketch of the Hillside Strangler. One time, on a tip from the lady across the street, Nick had even been picked up by the L.A.P.D. for questioning. Ironically, the typical role he played in the theatre he now had to act out in reverse; he had to convince his audience that he was *not* the bad guy.

It was at the Palomino Club, where Nick's fifties group and our trio were billed one night, that he told me of his crisis. He was tired of the music business, where mediocrities are marketed as rock stars and adulated by mindless groupies. He wanted out.

Even though he had just landed the lead in Man of La Mancha at a dinner theatre in Orange County, he was still unhappy.

"I feel bored and complacent. I need a real challenge," he said, over a glass of wine. "I've decided to take racing seriously. I've tried my hand at so-called honest jobs. It seems like the only profession where hypocrisy doesn't triumph is betting at the track."

It's one thing to make a profit at the track and another to make a living. The latter requires enormous increases in bet size. Most guys who've attempted the feat begin to erode from within. A player can be loose and free with $20 bets because they don't hurt. But at $200 a shot, decision making becomes poisoned by fear. The player is likely to think twice about betting the same type of high-yield longshot that would be an obvious investment at the twenty-dollar plateau. This fear is based to some degree on reason, since high-yield bets win less frequently. Although their long-term bottom line is superior, you can get killed in the short run.

I mentioned these things to Nick but he was dead set on his plan.

The next evening, our conversation shifted to Nick's place, where his wife, Lynn, was not thrilled about his horsebetting venture. She wanted to move to the suburbs, have children and pursue her commercial art work. It was as simple as that. Her identity crisis was parallel, in time, to Nick's, but contrary in substance.

Sonia and I were sitting in beach chairs on the cement sidewalk outside their first-floor apartment. The thick, sweet smell of jazmines everywhere. The drug pushers and drunks and low riders temporarily absent from view.

For Nick, drinking beer while sitting in cement surroundings was the closest thing to the stoop of a brownstone apartment in Brooklyn.

Meanwhile, Lynn, who had downed a can of beer, her normal limit, and was halfway through the next, was blunt about her anxieties.

"Next week, I'll be thirty-five," she said. "It seems about time to settle down. Soon it'll be too late."

While Lynn and Sonia chatted, Nick outlined his plans. He had just read two books by Beyer, books that Lynn thought should be burned by the Inquisition. Beyer's betting style was, as Nick would repeat, "to crush the race," and he was known to wager enormous amounts of money. He might bet a $500 exacta one way without reversing it. He could put $4,000 into multiple combinations of the twin trifecta.

Nick explained that the original Man of La Mancha, Don Quixote, had avidly read novels of chivalry, in which knights errant had gone off on fantastic journeys to kill giants and save damsels in distress. Seduced by his readings and against the protestations of his family, Don Quixote had decided to do, in real life, what the knights errant had done in fiction. It was a case of life imitating art. Friends and family in town did their utmost to protect Don Quixote from his folly, but to no avail.

Even in her exasperation, Lynn remained sweet and simple. She elaborated on the comparison between chivalry novels and Andrew Beyer books and insisted that Nick's attempt to convert a myth into reality was a folly just as mad as Don Quixote's.

It wasn't just a myth, Nick insisted, holding firm. His plan was to make an odds line for each potentially playable race. If his top choice was paying 3-1 and he gave it a 3-2 chance, he'd bet. If his top choice should have been 2-1 but was 3-2, he would pass this bet and consider his second choice. In other words, he was going to bet any contender that was paying off at least 50 percent more than his calculated fair return, and pass any other contender that did not meet these criteria.

Conceivably, he might have to bet his minimum $100 on his third most-likely winner if that one was paying better than fair odds at the same time that his first and second choices were bad bargains.

This method made lots of sense, but it was psychologically draining. There was a distinct statistical possibility for Nick to "pick" three winners in a row and lose all three races because the odds of those winners had been below fair value.

Psychological stress was not the only enemy. Time would also be a great menace. In order to make relatively objective odds lines, Nick would have to be there for every race, watch all the replays, make the long drive up Crenshaw and Highland Boulevard fighting the smog and traffic, then get to work tallying trainer stats, trip notes and key races.

Next, speed figures would have to be crunched out assembly-line style, as part of his preliminary handicapping. Then, at 7:30 the next morning, he would get the late scratches and do his serious handicapping. Timewise, few professions are so demanding. Practicing the guitar, writing new band arrangements, rehearsing a play, none of these rivals serious betting.

In the early days of Nick's betting odyssey, Lynn would ask each afternoon how he had done. Nick preferred talking about any subject but racing. He had set down some ground rules. Anything less than $200, win or lose for the day, was an insignificant amount. Only thousand dollar days, in the won or lost column, were worthy of more than passing comment.

Passing comments were all they had time for. Lynn once complained that this was worse than being a football widow. Nick countered that there was no comparison. Watching football games on TV was passive. Doing the races was active for both mind and soul. It was an exercise of the neurons; you never heard of cases where elder horseplayers became senile.

Occasionally I would shoot over Laurel Canyon to Nick's apartment and offer to chauffeur him to Hollywood Park. Not once did he let me drive. He wanted to be in control, zip in and out of traffic in his little MG. My driving was too slow, he said, too placid for dealing with the crazy drivers out there. Nick had learned to drive in New York, where taxis eat you up if you don't stand your ground. In a different juxtaposition of life, I might have been the slow guy in the fast lane that Nick was growling at with his thick eyebrows bent jaggedly toward the point between his eyes.

After a few weeks, Nick's personality began to change. He was so intense in his study of the toteboard, his adjusting of lines, that I had become a mere appendage. In his mind, I was still playing a game while he was involved in serious business.

While Larry and I sat up in the grandstand and enjoyed the afternoon, watching the planes descending over LAX, taking in the fresh green of the infield, Nick was down at the rail, never sitting, never remaining in one spot, moving into the eating area where he could stand at a table and do his calculations while sticking French fries in his mouth.

I saw Nick as an artist involved in an immense mural who needed vast territory to do his work. He might have been Picasso painting Guernica, a dead serious event. His sense of humor would still pop up occasionally, like the time when we were standing at the rail and one of the horses in the post parade crapped.

"It's a two-turd event," he said, an obvious play on words, since the race was going to be a "two-turn" event.

Or like the time when he had made two win bets in the same race, $100 each, since both fillies had attractive odds.

"I call this a menage-a-trois," he said, with a twinkle in his eyes.

But these light moments were becoming few and far between. I began to drift away from Nick, recognizing his need for the type of solitude that would nurture his intensity. He was in another league now, and I had to respect that.

In fact, I was proud of him. After having been down over a thousand in the first week, he had battled back and was now clearing a profit. None of his earlier setbacks made him waver.

One of the supreme tests of character came after a claiming race in which he had bet his second choice at 6-1, a horse Nick said "shoulda been 3-1." The 6-1 horse got blocked by a McCarron horse in front, and never had the chance to use his pent up energy. Meanwhile, Nick had not bet his top choice in the same race because his personal odds line said 2-1 and the horse was going off at 2-1.

There was no advantage. With no edge, you can't neutralize the track take, a tax of 17 percent off winning payoffs. In the last flashes, Nick's top choice had gone up to a bettable 3-1. He ran to put the bet in. The guy in front of him at the large transaction window was arguing with the teller. Nick got shut out. The horse won. Here was an example of the chaos theory in physics, where uncalculable nuances in movement affect outcomes. With a clear path on either bet, Nick would have won.

I expected that he'd take the loss hard. He shook his head once, then got back to business with the next race, as if he had just been checked hard against the brick wall, then returned to his skating position. Later, away from the track, he would explain to me that his lines had been underestimating the chances of his most-likely winners, a typical quandary with inexperienced line makers. He would make the adjustment.

"I just paid a little tuition," he said, "and learned a big lesson."

As the weeks went by, I socialized less and less with Nick at the track. He took his intensity back home so I stopped meeting him there, too.

From a distance I'd watch him after a big score. There was no rejoicing. And on those occasions when his horse lost by a nose, there was no griping, either.

Occasionally, Nick would phone me with a progress report. Our friendship continued only because it was he who determined when we could or couldn't interact. These periodic reports centered on his psychological stamina. His bankroll was growing, to be sure, but he was more concerned with his ability to cope with the stress. He would let me know on those occasions when he detected a dose of flakiness from within that threatened his decision making.

Such moments were especially menacing following a three or four-race losing streak. With each succeeding loss, it was tougher to slap down $200 on his second most-likely winner going off at 7-1, while bypassing a top choice that was no bargain.

He made an art of accepting defeat on those occasions when his unbet top choice would beat out a second choice he had bet.

"That means nothing in the scheme of things," he explained over the phone, which was now our only medium of communication. "It means more when my second choice pays $12 for $2 and I have $200 on him."

During the last week of the meet, I received a phone call from Nick. He explained that he had insured himself a profit for the meet but that he would need a big score in order to make that profit significant. "You'd never think that with all those races, it could boil down to just one race. But that's the way it is."

On the last day of the meet, in the expanding late afternoon shadow of the Hollywood Park grandstand, I was surprised to hear Nick calling me over as I stood at the rail to watch the post parade. Weeks had gone by since he had said a word to me at the track. Now he was showing me his program.

Warholic was Nick's most likely winner, going off at 9-5. Nick had him at 8-5. There was a minimal edge. Nick's second choice, Wood Carving, was flashing on the board at 5-1. Nick's estimated fair price was 3-1.

"This is the classic dilemma," he said, with a serenity I had not observed in him since the meet had begun. "I'm going to bet $200 on Wood Carving. If Warholic wins, so be it."

Nick had begun the meet as an amateur and was ending it as a professional. The storm within had subsided and his inner sea was calm. I knew that if Warholic or some unexpected third horse were to win, Nick was not going to lose his appetite. Nor would it be high-fiving time if Wood Carving were to win.

The race was never in doubt. On the far turn, you could see from their strides and the rhythm of their breathing that Wood Carving, the stalker, was going to wear down Warholic little by little and nail him before the wire. Wood Carving returned $12, which meant that Nick had cleared a thousand with his $200 bet.

At the end of the three-month meet, Nick and I got together for a beer on the beach chairs in his driveway. Deep into summer now, the jazmine aroma had dissipated. Even at dusk, some of the day's brutality was still embedded in the hot cement pavement. Nick shared with me that he had finished the three-month meet up five thousand. His tone of pride and accomplishment was remarkably subdued.

"I didn't get the chance to tell you before. Lynn and I decided to separate. I guess she deserves the chance to find her path," he said, without conviction.

In dry periods between gigs, I had done jobs at the divorce court on Hill Street. I knew that in most dissolution cases, the separation is good. In this case there were two good people who were simply not made for each other. She would be free to find her niche. At thirty-five, she needed to settle down, have kids.

Nick would be free to continue his quest. Clearly, he felt betrayed. But Nick was not the type of friend that you comfort with an "it'll be alright."

"Hey," I said. "It's the best thing for two good people with different dreams."

Nick could accept the intellectual side of it. But he admitted that he was hurt by the betrayal. When a man is engaged in a monumental struggle, and on the verge of winning it, his woman is supposed to stand by his side. That's the way it should be in the center of Hollywood.

I learned then that they had been separated for more than a month already. Nick had forged ahead in his struggle against the odds in spite of this major disruption in his life. I thought his triumph deserved a special asterisk:

*Continued intense concentration and maintained psychological stamina during stormy relationship.

I was reminded of a line from a Brecht poem: "They ate their food between massacres."

When it was time to leave, I got up and embraced him.

"Not many horse bettors can carry on with household problems. In fact, not many can do it with the burden of any household at all. That makes your triumph monumental. When Sonia and I have the slightest squabble, the past performances become as confused as the facade of an Aztec temple. I lose it."

"On the contrary," Nick said. "It wasn't Lynn who defeated our relationship. It was the ideals of the outside world. It's horse racing against the outside world. Playing the ponies becomes its own world and you get what you put into it. Not like anything else out there."

Nick found a smaller apartment in Arcadia, within walking distance of Santa Anita. I figured that once the Del Mar and Pomona meets ended, he'd be ready to get back to the only honest profession he knew.

I had decided to wait out the first week of Santa Anita's Oak Tree meet, gathering profiles of which running styles had the advantage, as well as which trainers were hot. I was playing the regular engagement at The Money Tree in North Hollywood, spending my mornings in bed, taking late afternoon walks with Sonia.

On Wednesday of the second week of Oak Tree, I drove out to Santa Anita and found a comfortable spot on the grass in the infield. I was there primarily for aesthetic reasons. The winds of the previous night had cleared the air. The rugged San Gabriel Mountains stood gloriously behind the backstretch. The downhill turf course, the only asymmetrical highlight of American racing, was a lush green, with deep pink bougainvillia spilling over nearby fences.

I would be making a few recreational bets and that was it. With my binoculars, I looked across the stretch, high up into the M section to see who was there. Al was there. So was Larry. And Gene. All my unemployed actor friends. Everyone except Nick. I even saw Charles Bukowski, seated alone at the end of the grandstand, in the U section, where the horses turn for home.

Perhaps Nick was down by the rail. I got up from my spot on the grass and went through the tunnel to look for him. He was not there. Nor was he in the eating area with the stand-up tables that served as his desks. None of the guys had seen him.

I left after the sixth and wheeled over to his new apartment.

"Hey, Matt, great to see you," said the unshaven Nick. "How come you're not at the track?"

"I was going to ask you the same thing."

"I'm taking a straight gig," he said. "I begin Monday."

"All the more reason you should be out at the track now. We could go back there and catch the ninth race trifecta."

"What use is one more day? I'll pass."

"What's this straight job?" I asked.

Nick was in the kitchenette, grinding the beans of a French roast. He took a whiff of the ground beans, then brewed me a cup of strong coffee. He knew what I liked without asking.

"Editor of a drama magazine."

It made no sense to me. Nick had rejected the back stabbing, influence peddling, ass kissing of the straight world, gone to the races and made a profession out of it, and now he was dropping it.

I didn't get it. A straight job was what Lynn would have wanted for him, yet she was gone, apparently forever. Nick wasn't doing this for Lynn.

I wanted to question his values. He had done an about-face on me, and more important, he had betrayed his own standards. Still, I felt uncomfortable in the role of values cop, moral policeman, so I just waited to see if he would bring up the subject himself.

Instead, he got to talking about his new brewing technique, one that makes the coffee taste just as good as it smells. I had never seen him so serene. He just might begin driving like a midwesterner. His dark eyes sparkled like the rich coffee.

I suspected that this tranquility was simply the eye of the storm. He would begin his job Monday, say no to the boss on Tuesday and get fired on Wednesday. Thursday he'd be back at the track with the same intensity as before.

I was wrong. In fact, he had begun to enjoy doing nothing. Perhaps that was something embedded in him since the old neighborhood in Brooklyn, where the art of hanging around was as highly sophisticated as it is in Paris or Barcelona.

It was easy to swing by to see him after the races, so I saw him regularly. I met Karin, his new girl friend. He had met her at the rail at Hollywood Park. Evidently, she was a recreational horseplayer.

While some people would be impressed by her natural beauty, which was not forced at all by Max Factor products, I was dazzled by the ease with which she moved from one task to another, the artful way she set down the tray of cheese and crackers.

One evening, when Sonia and Karin got into talking about spices and herbs, cilantro, cumin, ginger and the like, it gave me the opportunity to bring up the subject of the ponies with Nick.

"I know what you've been thinking, Matt," he said. "And I don't know what to say."

"But you proved it could be done, Nick," I said, censoring any words that might be interpreted as inquisitorial, but there remained a judgmental streak in the tone of my voice.

"Racing takes a lot outa you," he said. "It's like being an offensive tackle. One slip, just one moment of weakness, and the quarterback gets sacked and you've lost the game. You've got to be up for every single play! It takes too much outa you."

Nick was now only a brisk ten-minute walk from the track, with a woman who enjoyed the races. It hardly seemed the right time to quit.

Still, Nick was adamant in his decision. Racing had been his friend, but a very demanding friend.

Even though he had proven he could beat the races, he'd lost his passion for the game. I could see that if I was going to make it at the track, I would not only have to beat the game, but also find a way that was compatible with my own temperament.

71

The Numbers Crunchers

Somehow Nick's defection from racing renewed my own resolve to be a winner. But resolve is one thing and clarity another. My search for the right path was made more confusing by numbers crunchers like Derek Johnson.

Derek was standing up in the aisle after the seventh race at Santa Anita. His administrative job was just high enough in the insurance office hierarchy so that he could take off early and join Barry, Frank, Big Ed and me in the M section of the grandstand. He was talking of quitting his job and playing the horses full time.

He looked down on us and crowed about the refined pace figures that had helped him cash in on the last race, how he was now hitting 79 percent winners.

Derek was built like a tractor, his head a rotating cabin. He was scooping us up like so much landfill, and dumping us in the ditch. The trainer didn't matter, he said, which eliminated one of my favorite angles. Class didn't matter, which nullified Barry's comprehensive evaluation of each horse's proper place in the pecking order. The odds didn't matter, which buried Frank's line-making strategies.

I'd observed Derek as a winner, no matter what methodology he adopted. Never before had he resorted to such unbelievable monomania. "Only the numbers matter," he now concluded. His horse had just won the seventh race, paying $6.60.

Barry and Frank looked at each other with comic disbelief.

"If you'd only iron out the wrinkles," Frank teased, "you might get your hit rate up to 90 percent."

Derek didn't catch the sarcasm.

"I think you're right," he beamed.

Coming up were the eighth race on the grass and the ninth, a maiden event, where numbers were less reliable. Derek played neither of those more open-ended types of races, so he left, computer in arm.

In his wake, Barry reflected. "People like Derek can't handle ambiguity. That's why they go for shopping malls, artificial turf, dull symmetrical baseball stadiums and rigid numbers. But horse betting is a lot more challenging, more subtle than a hit rate or a bunch of numbers."

Barry had credentials. He was making his living at the track. But I found myself defending Derek.

"Derek's been a winner since the get-go. I've seen him..."

"Winners keep it to themselves. Only touts claim 79% winners. Your friend's a space cadet."

I recall Derek's words, a week later: "My numbers are so precise that I don't remember the names of the horses." His once jovial face had frozen into a permanent smirk.

"I don't know, Derek," I said. "I just don't think this game can be reduced to a single numerical determinism."

"Don't be El Primitivo, Matt. Join our group," he said paternally. "You still have time."

It was Big Ed, a tax accountant, who had first called me El Primitivo because of my reluctance to reduce the game to modern numbers. Like his nemesis the IRS, Ed, played by the numbers. A whole revolution of numerical handicapping methods was passing me by. I was an anachronism.

It began with Andrew Beyer, although Barry says it really began in the fifties when Walter O'Malley dressed the Bums up and moved them to L.A., to Chavez Ravine, strictly for finances.

The next time I heard from Derek was in print, a pamphlet proclaiming the ultimate truth in his figures. But these new figures, I noticed, were derived differently from the ones he had exalted that day in the M section. Why the need to revise a 79% method?

Months later, he hooked up with a computer handicapper, peddling seminars and high-priced software to a "select few," they said, so that they wouldn't hurt their odds. Derek's secret formula was once again revamped, suggesting that the figures from his book were also less than adequate.

It seemed as if the world around me was becoming infested with numbers crunchers, with the same kind of additive linear thinking that led to more lanes on more freeways with the traffic only getting thicker.

As friends like Derek turned into strangers, I was overcome with malaise. I sought comfort in my music, but to no avail. One night, I received a phone call from my agent, Phil. The sure-bet recording contract, he told me, had once again fallen through. The record company's excuse this time was our age. I was the youngest in the trio, at thirty-five, and even that was too old. James, the percussionist, had played with Ella, which made him almost a fossil.

"It's the demographics," Phil said. "The probability of marketing a group declines as the age of the musicians goes up."

"What about the music itself, Phil? If we had nothing new to say, you wouldn't be our agent! That's what you told us!"

"Record companies don't listen to the music anymore," he said, in a thick New York accent. "They've got software that projects what's gonna be a success. They've got their numbers, and that's what tells them what to do."

My malaise turned to desperation. Phil met with the three of us, Curtis, James and me, before our next gig at The Money Tree, to have a drink and regroup.

"I dunno what t'say," Phil moaned. "The talent scouts I used to count on now treat me like a stranger."

"It's the numbers crunchers," I said. "They're everywhere."

"What the fuck's the numbers crunchers," he asked.

I saw Derek, saw the freeways widening in the L.A. haze. I saw Derek again, bulldozing. I saw a record contract going under.

"I can't say what it is, but this numbers thing is hitting me from all sides," I confided. "It feels like an invasion."

"Great," Phil said. "Next thing you're gonna tell me is that some alien pods have landed, giving off pollen that turns people into numbers crunchers!"

"Hey Phil," Curtis said. "Matt's got a point. You know Roland, the homeboy who helped me with our arrangement of Afro Blues. Kid's brilliant. I tried to get him into the U.S.C. music program. They wouldn't let him in 'cause of his SAT score. One bad number and they won't give the homeboy a chance."

Phil scratched his balding head.

"Look, if you guys are tellin' me to give up, it won't work. I've got some leads in Europe. They worship jazz musicians over there. Lemme try to land you a spot, Paris or Milan. Maybe I can get a label over there to record you live. I ain't givin' up."

At that moment Big Ed came in, pulled up a chair, and set his Racing Form on the table. The red DRF logo immediately raised my spirits. After the last set, I would unwind by scanning the Form in search of hidden nuances, the same way I play the keyboard, beginning with the melody and basic harmony, then searching for that contrapuntal magic that digs deeper into the song.

After the first set, Ed cornered me. He had downed a couple of hard ones and his deep, thick voice had risen a few keys.

"Matt, I'm getting killed. Can you spare a half hour a day to go over the card? Brainstorming together, we might both boost the return on investment."

I was not thrilled about going over the card with Ed. He was a hard-headed listener. But I had no choice. He had been there when I needed him for tax advice. I'd have preferred to help him paint his house, or weed his garden, rather than listen to his application of speed figures.

After the last set, I drove home to a night of long, slow and sad love making to the tune of Billie Holiday's voice.

The next morning, I woke up and touched Sonia on her delicate temple, overwhelmed with a deep spirit of love and companionship. I thought how our life seemed stuck in neutral and wondered what had happened to our dream, our original plan to live in Europe for at least a year.

We had agreed, in principle, that money was replaceable but time could never be recovered. Deedee, Sonia's daughter by her ex, could learn French, while she was still young enough to pick it up. During our long evening walks, we had even worked out a strategy. We would cut down from two cars to one, rid ourselves of the possessions that were clogging up our life, find a cheap flight through the wholesalers, then take off.

With Sonia's high-pressured bank job leading to migraines and the record contract a dud, now seemed the ideal time to activate our plan.

"I've got it, Sonia. Wake up!"

She moaned.

"Are you listening? Your job's too tense, The Money Tree's a dead end. Now's the time for us to go."

"Where?"

"To Europe, of course!"

"Matt, you're talking crazy. In one more year I'll be vested. I'll qualify for a pension at retirement age."

"The job stress will kill you," I countered, "before you ever collect any retirement. That's why the banks can afford to offer such plans. They know that most of their employees won't live long enough to collect. They have the figures to prove it. Let them find a new trust administrator."

Sonia asked how I could just dump my house band job. I told her that the longer I remained cloistered between the oak panel walls of that cozy place, the less likely the outside world would ever hear my riffs.

"The numbers don't add up," she concluded. "We haven't saved enough. We have children. We can't throw away a pension, just like that."

Case closed. It seemed that Sonia too had become a numbers cruncher.

I could insist on our going to France and eventually I might wear her down. But the richest experiences in our relationship had come about through consensus. I needed her commitment. Stopping me was this invisible numbers conspiracy that now extended all the way into my own bedroom.

About noon I picked up Big Ed at his office on my way to the track. As soon as he got in, it felt like my small Civic was not roomy enough for the two of us. Big Ed was an eight-cylinder Buick kind of guy. He was suddenly intimidating. His size may have had something to do with it but the numerical wall around him was the main culprit. When he had asked me for help, he had not clarified that I was not allowed to tamper with his Figures. He was a composer who wanted to write a thousand songs without ever changing the three basic chords.

From our initial discussion of the card, I suspected he merely wanted me to confirm his opinions. Horse betting is such a solitary game that most players welcome a little confirmation from an informed source.

I drove into the Santa Anita lot. We began the long trek toward the gate through a sea of automobiles and stray thoughts. I longed for a European setting where unencumbered foot traffic still existed. No pedestrian had arrived at Santa Anita since 1977. Local colleges now offered campy Anthropology courses called Pedestrian Cultures 101.

As we went through the turnstyle and picked up our programs, Ed confided he couldn't handle losing streaks. Good figures kept him afloat. But even figures advocates like Beyer and Quinn had recognized, in print, that the average mutuel for figures play was on the decline, as more players got wind of the numbers.

Ed's numerical safety net provided a sense of security during the anticipation period before a race. Later, if the horse lost, at least Ed was comforted that he'd done his numbers correctly. But his figures analysis, more often than not, was like a construction bid that wins the contract before the inevitable cost overrun.

My research had proven beyond a doubt that a horse is far more likely to run a significantly different figure today than to run to the same figure again. Numbers predicted continuity, but change was a more likely outcome.

Still, Ed was a clever handicapper within the constricted boundaries he had set for himself. But he rarely made that big score needed for a significant profit. How could he if the public that determined the odds was doing the same thing he was?

We both passed the opener. It was one of those part-mist, part-smog days when you couldn't see the San Gabriel mountains behind the backstretch. The mist conjured up vague doubts.

Although Ed collected more often than I did, my return on investment was higher than his. But I had not reached the stage of self-confidence where one KNOWS that the next big score is inevitably on the horizon. I was not mature enough as a player to escape the self-doubt caused by losing streaks.

Not infrequently, Ed and I would walk out of the track, he a winner and I a loser. Filled with self-doubt, I questioned my approach. If Ed's figures were applied with all their nuances, they could be successful, like a three-chord pop song.

And Sonia, too, might be right about her pension. We both had children by our previous marriages. Should we leave L.A., I'd still be responsible for the child support, Sonia would say good-bye to her high salary and benefits, and I would be dropping a steady gig at The Money Tree. My point of view seemed riskier, more impressionistic. Still, in Paris jazz *was* popular. Surely I could find a niche there to support us. And they had eight race tracks around that city, the sign of true culture!

In the second race, Ed eliminated a filly I thought was a contender. Her speed figure in her last race was too low to compete with these. She was the two-horse, Karla's Kat.

Ed was a member of MENSA, the organization of the high IQs. (MENSA members generally don't know that their moniker means "dumb" in Mexican Spanish.) I thought that his intelligence gave me a shot at deprogramming him from his numbers dependency. Karla's Kat could prove to Ed that numerical determinism is an illusion.

"Your figs make no sense here, Ed. Karla's Kat was racing on a sloppy track. She's bred to hate the slop! You gotta excuse that race."

"I subtracted the negative variant from her raw figure," he countered. "She's still too damn slow."

Supposedly, the variant tells you how slow the track was running that day, by averaging how much slower the times are compared to a normal day of racing. But the variant is an average. Some horses are adversely affected by an off track. Others actually like it. Each case is unique.

"It's not enough to subtract the negative variant," I argued. "Karla's Kat couldn't handle the footing; that race should not even count. Go back further in the past performances."

"How far back you want me to go?" he asked, exasperated.

"She's got excuses in her last four. You'll have to go back five races."

"You can't do that. It's too far back."

Here is one problem with numbers crunching. On too many occasions, no race or races is typical enough to be used

79

for a projected "figure". When this happens, you have to resort to logic; if a horse has proven capable of winning at today's class level, then he is a contender, figure or no figure. But the numbers crunchers often prefer to use a bad number rather than no number at all.

I was in a double bind. Ed had asked me to help him. But because of his steadfast commitment to his figures, I might as well have been writing to my congressman. I was talking to the Rock of Gibraltar. At the race track I'd walked away from guys like this a hundred times. But this was Ed, a good friend who would break his back for me.

Partly out of spite, I got up, went under the grandstand and put ten bucks to win on Karla's Kat at 15-1. I had argued simply that you couldn't eliminate the filly on the basis of figures. I didn't even know whether I liked her to win the race. Had I not been engaged in the polemic with Ed, I'd have never bet her. I had wagered ten bucks not on a horse but on my point of view.

The six furlong race began on the backstretch, in the mist. Karla's Kat got off cleanly and was stalking the two leaders.

Around the turn, she swept by the front runners and grabbed the lead. Sorenson hit her harder. At the wire she got caught by two closers, finishing only 3/4 of a length from the victory.

Karla's Kat had proven my point. She had nearly won! Yes! It was better to use no number at all than a badly conceived number.

"You see, Matt!" Ed said. "Karla's Kat lost the race; she wasn't fast enough."

"Whaddya mean? She just ran a winning race! Your figs had'er 15 lengths behind! She lost by less than a length! Put Stevens on her instead of Sorenson and she wins, bad figures and all!"

My voice was booming. The whole grandstand was staring at me, I thought, as if I were the typical sore loser. It took me five races to calm down.

The day's feature, a mile and a quarter on the dirt, was the most bettable race on the card, with horses shipping in from all over the country.

"I pass," Ed said. "Most of these haven't run the distance. They've got no race over the track. There's nothing to compare."

In races where everything is comparable, you rarely get a good price on a horse. "Nothing to compare" means a chance to make money on a 10-1 that should be 3-1.

"What about the breeding?" I asked. "Why not see if any of these are bred to get the mile and a quarter?"

"It's a pasadena," he smiled. "There's other races that lend themselves better. Too much uncertainty here."

"Too much uncertainty, Matt," Sonia had also told me. "You want us to give up a steady income."

Ed and Sonia were singing the same refrain.

To me there was more risk and uncertainty in Sonia's remaining on the job because she often came home from work looking like a filly who's just been whipped mercilessly through the stretch.

But, petite Sonia was tough inside. One to two said she'd overcome the stress factor, 2-1 said she wouldn't. My intuitive wagering line gave a 33 percent chance that today's stress would kill her before she could collect on her pension. But I had no numbers to prove it.

"Where do you get your odds?" she asked.

"From right up here," I said, pointing to my head. "You want numbers, I'll give 'em to you."

Like Ed, Sonia's sense of security resided in the numbers. Numbers on a salary, a pension, a life insurance policy. Her father had died when she was four. Her mother had lost interest after that. Sonia had fended for herself. With little support, she had taken command of her own life, acquired an adult concept of responsibility before she had reached puberty.

Growing up vulnerable, her protection was in being responsible. Throughout her childhood, she had never missed a homework assignment. No matter how meaningless the task, she did it. The grades gave her confidence. They could be measured. Now, she was performing meaningless assignments for a bank. She knew that she was throwing away eight hours a day but what choice did she have?

"Look at it this way," I argued. "You're talking about a pension that will only be a hundred a month if you stay on the job one more year. Then, you'll want more pension, so you still won't quit. How about doing something for yourself for a change?"

While I hammered away with my intuitive projections, she responded with tangible figures. I groped for a way to rekindle her spirit of adventure. I didn't want to look back, thirty years later, and say, "we should have done it when we had the chance."

I recalled my old man, churning out statistical tallies of atomic particles. He loved Mozart. Had he put a little of Mozart's Forty-first into his physics, perhaps he'd have broken the barrier that prevents craft from becoming inspiration.

Back with Big Ed at Santa Anita, the mist still shrouded the San Gabriel Mountains. I was intrigued by a colt in the feature, Sham's Ego. His daddy, Sham, had produced lots of long-distance winners. More important, as a grass sire, Sham's record was dubious. The switch from turf to dirt would be advantageous. Sham's Ego had been forced into the wrong lifestyle. Now he would run free. I gave it one last chance with Ed.

"Look here, Sham's Ego was an early speed horse in Europe. Europe discriminates against that running style. America favors it. He might wake up today."

"Clever, clever," Ed said, "but the colt's never raced on the dirt so we have nothing to measure."

Ed was right. There was no figure. But the non-countable evidence made Sham's Ego a contender. The odds said the rest. At 8-1, anyone who backed him would be more than compensated for the uncertainty of no comparable figures. Ed didn't see it that way.

"I'll always love you, Big Ed," I said. "But don't ever ask me again to help you with your handicapping. I'd rather go over to your house and pull weeds, or anything else."

"What can I say, Matt? What you're doing may be interesting, but it ain't handicapping."

Sham's Ego broke alertly. He galloped just off the pace. On the backstretch, he overtook the front runner. The pace was slow, allowing Sham's Ego to conserve energy. At this point, the crowd would have taken him at even money. I had him at 8-1.

He drew off in the stretch. I had won a chunk thanks to the uncertainty factor.

Meanwhile, Ed was even for the day, his self-confidence undented. If one day, there were no good numbers to measure races, Ed would simply give up horse betting and play cards at the Gardena Poker Club.

After dropping Ed off at his house in Glendale, I stopped at the North Hollywood library and photocopied a few statistical articles on stress-related illness. Sonia wanted some certainty in her life. I was going to convince her, with figures, that there was only insecurity in her remaining under heavy stress for another year, that her "vested" numbers were deceiving.

Like Sham's Ego, Sonia and I were functioning in the wrong context. We would do well to ship ourselves to another continent.

It was showdown time. We ate leftovers. Sonia added three aspirins to the mix. During our evening walk, I elaborated on my library statistics. "Each new day on your job, Sonia, is two days less of your life, one today and one on the back end. Drop it and let's go."

"Matt, I want to go too. But I've done all the figures, air fare, housing, food—not even counting entertainment because you say just being there is entertainment—and we need to come up with about twelve thousand to stay for a year."

"Deedee's gonna learn French," I countered. "That counts for twelve thousand in tuition in an L.A. French school. In France, our daughter becomes bilingual for free. Here it costs us at least twelve thou, with no assurance she'd become fluent."

"Even if you're right about gigs over there, Matt," Sonia said, "we'll still need six thousand before we can go. That's the minimum. And that assumes you'll make more once we're there!"

"We will. Don't I always pull a rabbit out of the hat?"

"We have no working papers."

"We won't need any. Musicians get paid under the table all the time."

It was a quiet neighborhood of million dollar houses. Our voices, mainly my voice, had given the dogs something to bark about. I tried to emphasize our solidarity.

"Sonia, we're besieged. Both of us. It's the shit syndrome. People take shit until it doesn't bother them anymore. We never intended our life to become a balance sheet. Sometimes you have to take a chance."

We turned back. The aroma changed from eucalyptus to magnolia. We were the only pedestrians. I sensed we were passing fortresses. Somewhere behind those fortress windows, faces peered out at us. It was then that Sonia made me an offer I couldn't refuse.

"I have an idea, Matt," she said. "Remember when I backed you with a fifty dollar bankroll at the track and you turned it into a new stereo? Well, I'll back you with a five hundred dollar bankroll now and let's see if you can turn it into six thousand."

"That's a lot of money in a short time!"

"Just bet more."

The challenge was invigorating. I was flattered by her confidence in me. But she was asking me to make a thousand percent profit. A mix of fear and adrenaline rushed to my head.

"You're asking of me something that your banker friends would find impossible."

"You did it with the fifty dollars! If you want us to go to France. Make it happen."

The stereo incident had been a lucky stroke. When I first got to know her, I discovered that my gambling culture was more foreign to her than Nepal or Bangladesh. The only bridge was the comparison between horseplayers and bankers. I remember her words: "...but bankers don't lose the principal."

She had given me fifty dollars so that I could demonstrate how it worked. I went on a binge. Two things had worked in my favor. I had been feeling very positive about myself, and I didn't have to make that much, percentage-wise to outperform the bankers. With such a small stake, I could make minimal bets, totally eliminating the fear factor. Within two weeks, with luck along the way, I had made the bankroll grow seven times over.

Now, things were different. But for Sham's Ego, I'd be down for the meet. As it was, I was struggling to stay even. My self-assurance was near its record low. The recording contract had fallen through. Of greater impact was the aura of the numbers crunchers; the more mediocre my own play, the more my subconscious tended to believe their hype.

If they'd been limited to the race track, I suppose I could have dealt with them. But it seemed as if everything around me was controlled by them. Watching smart friends like Ed switch to the other camp had unraveled my sense of command.

This was one of the few things I could not explain to Sonia. To her, any investment is a mechanical decision. What did self-assurance have to do with betting the best horse in the race?

On the other hand, I had often performed best when backed to the wall. It took me a minute and eleven seconds to accept her challenge. In fact, at that moment, if some stranger had walked up to me and handed me six thousand dollars to go to Paris, it would have been a letdown. I had always wanted to be a professional player. Here was my opportunity.

My walking pace picked up. I was energized by a challenge that included not only a huge return-on-investment requirement, but a severe time constraint. It was the end of April. Deedee's school ended in early June. Sonia reasoned that we'd have to leave as soon as school was out. She made sense. If Deedee was to attend school in France, she'd need three prior months of practice in the language. The earlier we arrived the better.

If we were going to leave by mid-June, we'd have to give notice to our landlord by mid-May, as well as make reservations by that time to qualify for a discount flight. That meant about two and a half weeks to convert $500 into $6,000.

Opening day, Hollywood Park, April 27, was my first test. My plan was to avoid becoming intimidated by the numbers crunchers' unyielding arrogance. But I could not attack them head on.

I defined my strategy as guerrilla handicapping. The only way to defeat the standing army was to strike when I had the advantage. I had to wait out all races where the solution might reside in the figures. To win those races, I'd have to become like *them*. Even if that proved successful, the percentage of profit in store would fall far short of my $6,000 goal.

By the last race, I was down seventy bucks. I saw three contenders in the maiden race. My top two choices were too low on the board. My only possible bet was my third most-likely winner, a first-time starter by the name of Claim, who was going off at 10-1.

Here was a classic case for the Gambling Shrinks. Down for the day, could I summon the courage to bypass my first and second choices, knowing that I wouldn't be playing the most likely winner? Big Ed, who was up for the day, badgered me about the unpredictability of maiden races. I wavered, betting only $10 to win. The psychology of vulnerability had taken its toll.

Claim took the lead and walked away from the field. After the first furlong, I would have donated my gall bladder to have the chance to put down more money. The day ended on the plus side, but only good enough for cigarette money had I been a smoker.

I needed a change of ambience. Curtis used his influence to get me a free room in Las Vegas. I took the Greyhound, studying Friday's card on the bus. I arrived just in time to get down on Jokers Jig, at the Barbary Coast race book. The maiden, claimed by Mitchell from its prior race, galloped home first by ten lengths, improving his speed rating by 20 points. I got 4-1 and thought I was invincible. From then on, the only correct decision I made was to stay away from the hookers who lived in my hotel.

Once more, my back was to the wall. In a ho-hum claiming race at Hollywood Park, on Sunday, two hours before my return ride to L.A., I noted an early speed bias and keyed in on my third choice, aptly named Iffy Iffy, in the exactas, combining him with everything else that could walk. Once more, it took guts to use a third choice that was offering the best payoff. The exacta came in and I was up $350 for the trip.

Once back in L.A., the bankroll expanded to $1,600 with two Matlow first-time starters, a Jacque Fulton tote-action horse and a turf horse named Cannon Bar that produced a $179 exacta. No figures methodology could have picked any of these winners.

On the other hand, my bankroll was not climbing fast enough precisely because I was obligated to pass so many races for fear of confronting the figures players head on.

On Sunday, May 8, I discovered an angle. Rafael's Dancer, a Michael Whittingham horse, was trying the grass for the third time after two flops. This was an entry-level allowance race in which none of the horses belonged and none were bred for the grass.

What intrigued me about Rafael's Dancer came from my memory, which normally excludes birthdays and anniversaries in order to allow room for odd bits of information about horses. The grass races where he'd failed came prior to the ten most recent past performances listed in the Form. As a result, I knew something the public didn't. Rafael's Dancer had lost two grass races, yes, but they had been classy stakes. In one of those races he had been fanned eight wide on the first turn, a more than legitimate excuse.

If you compared the horses he would be running against today on the basis of past speed or pace numbers, Rafael's Dancer did not figure. However, the comparisons weren't valid, since they were based on dirt races.

I was sitting with Frank and Ed. Frank published an iconoclast poetry magazine; he regarded against-the-grain handicapping as a genre of poetry. Ten minutes to post, Ed griped.

"I can't see how anyone can play a race like this. The numbers can't be compared."

Frank laughed.

"You wanna do arithmetic, Ed, don't come to the race track."

Frank was much less tolerant of Ed than I was. If Rafael's Dancer were to lose, a distinct possibility, Frank would have no hard feelings. He'd already cashed in on several of my longshots.

"Ed," I explained. "No one is saying this horse is an automatic winner. But you gotta believe that 18-1 is more than a fair price if you consider the logic."

"Logic doesn't win horse races."

It was a conversation between hedonists and puritans. The exchange had little to do with horse racing and much to do with the way opposite cultures viewed the world.

Across the grandstand of Hollywood Park, thousands of numbers addicts were tallying up dirt times and trying to apply them to a grass race. Ed knew better. He would not get caught in the ambush of guerrilla handicappers like Frank and me.

I bet $20 to win, $20 to place on Rafael's Dancer. My "logic" was too thin to make this a larger bet. But I did add another twenty in exactas, combining my choice with two other horses; the exactas were paying off at above a thousand apiece.

When they broke from the gate, Solis decided to hug the rail and save ground, the opposite of Rafael's Dancer's previous unsuccessful trip on the turf. The risk was that, galloping behind horses, Rafael's Dancer might run into traffic in the middle of a big move and be shut off.

Mercifully, around the last turn, the rail path opened like the Red Sea. But then just as quickly it began to close up, threatening to slam Rafael's Dancer into the rail and bury my sixty bucks.

Fortunately, Solis got him through the narrowest of openings and once clear, Rafael's Dancer burst ahead. The only way he could lose was by tripping or bolting over the rail. I was overcome with wonder. Here was my destiny in France, about to be determined by a dumb, thousand pound animal. As he extended his lead, I was possessed with self-loathing. Had I tripled my investment, Rafael's Dancer would have brought me within reach of my destiny. Why had I wavered?

One hope still remained. There was a three-horse photo for second in the exacta. I wanted them to put the two up, or the seven, for my $1,000 bonus. With Frank's sharp eyes, I didn't need to wait for the camera.

"Who's second, Frank? Who got the place?"

"Sorry, Matt. The five got it. I saw the head bobs."

Instead of delighting in a $600 score, I castigated myself for not having added the 5 to my exactas because I only had one week left to reach my $6,000 goal and I was still $3,800 short.

"I shoulda bet more," I said, dejected.

"Don't get greedy, my friend," Ed said. "You were skating on mighty thin ice with that selection."

For once, Frank agreed with Big Ed. "The only thing you had to go on was the trainer intention. That's not enough for a prime bet. You're being too hard on yourself. Be careful or you'll burn out like Nick."

I tend to be that way. On winning days, I feel inadequate. On losing days I pat myself on the back.

"With an 18-1 score," Ed added, "I'd be a helluva lot happier than you!"

"I need to win six thousand, not six hundred," I explained.

As we left, Ed put a sympathetic arm around me.

"Shit, if you could pick that godforsaken horse, you'll find a way to make it to France. That's what I say!"

At dinner that evening, Sonia offered some good news. Phil, our agent, had called. He'd gotten us a gig at a small night club called La Chene Noir, in Avignon, in the south of France. He felt, with this contact as bait, he'd be able to lure a few other jobs, perhaps in nearby Arles or Nimes.

The next week passed by with no bettable insights emerging, no matter how hard I dug into the past performances. I even resorted to figures analysis, only to come up with the consensus favorite. I felt foolish waiting in the hills, passing whole cards with my deadline approaching, but it would have been even more foolish to play a race where I had no edge.

Sunday the fifteenth was my last chance, with dark days on Monday and Tuesday. I could only find one bettable race where the co-favorites both looked like they were tailing off in form, in spite of their high speed figures. It was do or die time.

I knew, sooner or later, I'd have to deal with betting above my comfort level. I would have preferred to choose the perfect moment. But in racing, there never is a perfect moment. I had been prepared to put a hundred into the race. But if I won and came up short anyway, I'd be chastising myself for a long time to come. I learned that from Rafael's Dancer.

I went up to the large transaction window and put a $200 win-place bet on the three-horse, at 10-1, and another hundred on the five, at 8-1. I added a ten-dollar exacta box, for a total investment of $520. As usual, I had chosen a turf race. Either winner alone would not get me to my $6,000 goal, but the exacta would put me over the top.

In the stretch, both the three and the five were closing through traffic. The three took up slightly, while the five captured the lead. I'm not the type to get nervous during a horse race. One race doesn't mean a great deal in the long run. But now there was no long run. My heart was thumping like galloping hooves.

It had all come down to this. In deep stretch, the five-horse was trying to hold off the eight, who was closing on the outside, while my three-horse had finally gotten through on the rail, recovering his momentum. But it was the eight that had the final burst. My exacta finished second/third, with both my horses within a length of the lead. In the photo, the three-horse was second and paid $6.00 so at least I had made eighty dollars on the race.

There were three races left on the card. I desperately searched for some insight that would make me more knowledgeable than the crowd. I could find nothing. The temptation was there to take a stab, but I resisted.

I left Hollywood Park by way of the rail. Looking up at the immense grandstand, I wondered how I was going to deal with coming up short. Folks would ask me what I was and I'd say "horseplayer and musician," or "musician and horseplayer." The horseplayer part of me was bruised. Why was it that numbers crunchers like Derek, even like Big Ed, never seemed to suffer similar wounds?

In my mind, I went over my records for the meet. Most of my profits had come from smaller bets. Had I just bet the same amount on every race, regardless of how strongly I felt for my choice, I'd have been up another thousand!

Sonia would only see that I'd come up short. Guerrilla handicapping had not allowed me enough ambushes. I had not discovered a method with which I could confront the figures players head on. Still, I had made a third of the required amount. I'd need to convince her that we were now considerably nearer our goal, and that with the potential gigs and the eight race tracks surrounding Paris, we would make up the difference.

That night, we left Deedee with Sonia's sister and the two of us went to The Money Tree. During the first set, Big Ed came in and sat at Sonia's table.

After the set, I joined them. By then, Big Ed had downed a couple of hard drinks.

"You know what I told Sonia, Matt," he said, loosened up by the alcohol. "I told her that anyone who could pick Rafael's Dancer deserves to go to France."

Sonia explained that there were still budgetary problems.

"Anyone who can pick Rafael's Dancer will find a way to make money in France," Ed repeated.

Sonia smiled, said that she'd think about it. Her voice sounded like Ella's, the faint hint of sugar, the satiny texture.

For the second set, Hazel joined us. She'd sung with us before, with a deep husky voice a la Carmen McRae. Could she do any Jacques Brel? I asked. She did "Please Don't Go Away," one of Sonia's favorites.

Between sets, Sonia looked up at me, her big eyes shining. "It was beautiful, Matt." She sang a verse, *"ne me quitte pas, ne me quitte pas."*

"Just say the word," I said, "and you can hear that stuff every night in Paris."

"Remember there's no entertainment in our budget." Her voice mixed two overtones, one of scolding, one of solidarity.

"Unless Phil lines up some more jobs. Once the foot's in the door, the odds project in our favor. One gig leads to others."

"Okay, Matt," Sonia surprised me. "Let's do it!"

The phrase 'let's do it' sounded like a decision to have Chinese food or to go to the movies. I let her continue.

"Right now," she said, "with our rental deposit and if we sell both cars, we'll have enough for four, maybe five months. If we run out of money then, we'll just come back. Anyone who can pick Rafael's Dancer deserves a chance to see what he can do in France."

THE OTHER WOMAN

Paris. It was one of those chilly June evenings when sunlight lingers well beyond 10:00 p.m. Vince and I were riding on a bus through the Vincennes Forest, on our way back to our neighborhood near the Pere-Lachaise Cemetery.

I knew little about Vince, except that he was a New York boy with a French Trotskyite wife and the working papers that came with her, and that he had gotten me work with his chamber group because I'd given him an entertaining blow-by-blow account of a Mets-Dodgers game in which Dave Kingman had hit three homers, the last one in the top of the 14th to win it for the Mets.

We were both drunk that afternoon, in a tilting stone-walled bar near Place Vosges, and I think I got the story wrong, because now that I remember, Kingman was actually playing for the Cubs at the time. Americans like Vince can survive in Paris just fine, but a good baseball story gives them nostalgia for the good old U.S.A.

Before meeting Vince, it looked as if our plans were falling neatly into place. Right off the plane, I had a week of gigs down in Provence and hit a big exacta at an OTB cafe. But after a few exacta combinations finished last and next-to-last, I realized that I would need some serious schooling at the races. More ominous, in France accomplished jazz pianists were in great abundance and night club owners were not knocking at my door.

Vince had come along at the right time, just when our situation was deteriorating. Sonia had been cautioning me on a daily basis that we were dipping too quickly into our meager savings and we might soon have to return to the States. A letter from Brenda grilling me about a late child support payment added more gloom to the outlook.

The gig with Vince was a definite step down because we were playing in the Metro, depending on the generosity of strangers. The old clarinet(relic from my high school band days) that Sonia had insisted I tote along to Paris, "just in case," against my protests, was now serving me well as my underground tool.

Anyhow, the two of us were now headed home and the bus driver, a Jackie Gleason look alike, must have been ahead of schedule because he chose not to pass a Renault that was crawling in front of us. In fact, the whole scene played out in slow motion, as if some grand transmission had shifted the world into a slower gear.

In the dim, mellow light at the side of the road were the usual streetwalkers. They were leaning on cars parked in dirt inlets intermittently spaced between tall trees. The rancid smell of their perfumes reached the bus.

"I gotta get off," Vince suddenly said.

"What do ya mean?" I asked. I was sitting in the aisle seat.

"Never mind," he insisted. "Just move over. I gotta get out."

My usual passive self was about to yield to Vince's high-strung demand. But he seemed addled and that worried me. What if he disappeared? Without him, there'd be no gig, and no regular income. The Chatelet station where we played may not have been L'opera but it had the richest acoustics and the best tippers in the whole Paris underground. And no one down there asked to inspect my non-existent working papers.

"Come on, Matt, move over. I got to get laid," Vince grunted, as he began to push me out of his way.

"Not here," I grabbed him. "You don't know what you're getting into."

The eyes of the passengers around us were suddenly torn between our little drama and the glitzy spectacle outside. These were some exotic lookers out there. Not the usual whores.

The man next to me was no longer Vince the violinist. The fingers that grabbed my shirt and shook me loose were not the ones that slid the bow delicately over sensitive strings. He was too strong for me.

"Those are transvestites," I warned. "They're cross dressers looking for some strange trade. I come through here all the time on my way home from the trotters. I assure you there's no pussy out there. If you don't believe me, go on man, you'll find out the hard way."

When you're in a non-English speaking country, you figure you can say damn near anything and no one will understand you. But that's not the case, especially if you're saying something potentially embarrassing. A woman's voice touched us from behind.

"He is right," she said. "They are transvestites. That's why they look so perfect."

Both of us turned back to look at the sweet-talking woman. Like many French women, she wore no makeup; yet she was sensuous in an elusive way, with small but bright eyes. What a contrast between her and the gaudy female personas outside!

Confronted with both our opinions, Vince changed his mind and we continued on our way. Once off the bus, there was still a Metro to take. Vince was silent the whole time. We both lived near the Pere-Lachaise Cemetery, hangout of the Jim Morrison cult. Unable to contain my curiosity any longer, I prodded Vince for an explanation.

"Alright, Vince. Come clean. What's the story?"

Vince said he was a sex addict. He had to have it. The more pussy, the better. Periodically he'd go on a night-long binge, in one of the whore hangouts of Saint-Denis. Once, when living in Chicago, he'd split from a orchestra gig, taken a plane to El

Paso, walked over the bridge to Juarez, then began fucking everything in sight for over a week in "Boys' Town."

"Why the need for whores?" I asked. "You're a good lookin' guy. Why not real women? Like the one behind us in the bus."

Vince got impatient.

"I don't think you understand. Basically I'm a nymphomaniac. It's my addiction. I don't have time for the human part of it, for beating around the bush, sitting in dumb movie theatres for two hours, eating in restaurants and all that courting shit. I'm just after the pussy. That's it. Look, Matt. I need help. I don't want to blow my marriage. I've already ruined one, and squandered an inheritance. The only thing I got left is Dominique."

With my attention fixed on Vince's story, I nearly stepped in a pile of dogshit. In Paris, you learn to look down instead of up when you're walking. Too bad, since the best part of the city is up above: the odd, angular top floors of old apartment buildings, the cornices, the turrets, the sculpted stone, the art nouveau window frames.

"Look, Vince, I have an idea. Maybe I can help. How about we get together tomorrow, at 11:00 and talk it over. I'm not promising anything. But it might work. Right now I got to go."

By the time I left Vince it was 10:30 and the street lamps glowed. The city had changed from pewter grey to its gaudier, more fashionable night dress. I walked by a cabaret and heard the moan of a saxophone, wishing I was the one blowing in the small club and getting paid, not the one depending on Vince.

My idea for helping Vince might not work, but at least it was based, like most good ideas, on a serendipitous incident. Back in my horseplaying days in L.A., my neighbor Willy, when I first met him, had been an alcoholic. He was from a rural Mexican background. He worked a night shift at a factory and drank by day. One afternoon I took him to Hollywood Park. Willy was not too interested in studying the past performances. But he knew horses. We hung out at the rail. He was happy there.

The next morning, Willy knocked on my door, asked if I was going to the track. Within a few weeks of racing, Willy had become a regular and had memorized most of the horses on the grounds. Although he bought the Form, he rarely used it. Sticking to the basic program, he gave me his analysis.

"I remember Pyramid Zotz. He was washy last time. He went four wide. This time he's looking good."

Pyramid Zotz won the race.

I can't say that Willy was making big bucks out there. But he held his own. Some time later, I was playing catch with his son in the parking-courtyard of a one-floor apartment building.

Willy's wife opened her front door to call the kid in for homework.

"Matt, I want to thank you," she said in broken English. "Since Willy been going to the races, he stop drinking."

Horse racing as therapy had not been a conscious plan. It just materialized and worked with Willy. Maybe it would work with Vince. He could substitute a harmless but demanding passion in place of a destructive one.

But I didn't want to force the issue or make it too abstract. I wanted to avoid explaining what I was doing. Let it unfold, the way it had with Willy. Who knows, had I said to Willy, "the racing is a substitute for the drinking," it might not have worked.

Although the City of Paris had granted our chamber group the prime spot in the large vestibule connecting the stairways to the 1 and 4 Metro lines, we had to share the location. On Saturdays, Mondays and Wednesdays, an Andean music group took over. So Saturday was an ideal day to go racing with Vince.

We met at the OTB cafe by the Charonne Church. Lots of cafes in Paris don't have names, and this one didn't either. It was just a cafe, with stain glass windows depicting scenes from the neighborhood. It had a marble-based counter with a varnished wood rim and a mosaic top, and lots of cigarette butts on the floor.

We stood at the counter and sipped our espresso, the national beverage. At the tables, most of the people, including a few women, were studying their *Paris-Turf* racing forms.

"Okay," Vince said, "so tell me about your idea, your plan for helping me."

"We're not gonna talk. We're gonna do," I replied.

Vince didn't like that. He wanted to know what my plan was.

We were overwhelmed by the thick "blue" cafe smoke so I gave the barman three extra francs for a sidewalk table even though it was raw and cloudy out there, like most June days in Paris. At the table next to us, a man with a thick Arabic accent told a companion that he liked the seventeen-horse in the feature. At the doorway was an African woman in a long patterned dress, a baby wrapped behind her back. She filled out a trifecta ticket.

Once settled outside, I decided to tell Vince my plan. It was easier than arguing with him. And who knew? Maybe he was the type who needed to have the abstract up front before dealing with the concrete. I explained Willy's case history, said we were going to Saint-Cloud race track after I gave him an intro to the *Paris-Turf* past performances.

Saint-Cloud is on the other side of Paris, the fashionable west side, in a town across the Seine just beyond where the river curls north from the Eiffel Tower.

The track there is asymmetrical, shaped like an immense triangle. The stretch goes slightly uphill. Past the finish line, the jockeys flash their pink, turquoise, or black and yellow silks against a lush green background, as the horses take long, easy strides into some tall trees that stand right on a grassy chute. No wonder Degas watched the races the same way he saw ballet dancers.

Vince's dark eyes lit up. He was intrigued. This was an alternative to the solemn 12-step programs he'd experienced back in the States.

Down the Metro staircase, I explained that this was no quick fix. If he lost large amounts at the races, the therapy could be as bad as the disease. And with the 29 percent takeout in France, it was not easy to beat the game. It wasn't easy anywhere.

As we left the Opera stop, I made the comparison between handicapping and jazz improvisation. If you read the Form strictly according to the melody, you end up singing the same tune as the rest of the bettors. The pari-mutuel system, a French invention, penalizes those who invest with the crowd.

After two months of slowly depleting my bankroll, I thought I had come up with a couple of methods that the public didn't use. One was good old American pace handicapping. Since the running lines were explained in narrative, pace analysis was literally between the lines of the past performances.

My other technique involved premeditated dissonance. Each day, there's a feature race that is used in a national, off-track wager, called the "tiercé," where you've got to pick the top three finishers. Pick them in order, you win big. If you land it out of order, you collect a consolation.

For the "tiercé" races, now extended to "quarté" and "quinté," there's a four-page centerfold in the *Paris-Turf* that includes each trainer's opinion about his horse. With frankness unheard of among their American counterparts, French trainers state the current condition of their horse, how it's been working out, whether the intention is to go all out today or whether the horse has not yet peaked.

During my two months of racing, I was betting the minimum ten francs a pop, tuition money, and keeping meticulous records of trainer comments. Ninety per cent of the trainers were telling the truth. They weren't predicting outcomes, only saying that their horse was ready or not ready to run at its peak.

Where I expected to make money was with those trainers who were lying. I had thus far isolated three trainers who had deceived the public about their horses. One of them, Clotard, was entering La Coiffeuse in today's fifth.

"With this comeback race I expect to prepare La Coiffeuse for her agenda of jumping races," was the quote from Clotard.

In the past performances, La Coiffeuse's races prior to the layoff were of the steeplechase variety. So it superficially made sense what Clotard had said. But, since the French past performances are conceptual, not just chronological, there's an insertion of each horse's most comparable race. The bottom race listed for La Coiffeuse was from the previous year and showed a victory at Saint-Cloud, at the same 1,600 meter mile distance over the flat.

Captivated, Vince grilled me with questions, but I had to show him by example rather than by word. The passion I wanted to pass on to him was for investing, not for gambling, for analysis, not for compulsion. By not making a bet during the first four races, I hoped Vince would catch on.

Now, all I needed was for La Coiffeuse to run a decent race. We bet on her win-place. (Place, in France, means finishing in the money, first, second or third.)

With the crowd seeing the layoff, seeing that La Coiffeuse was a jumper who should be racing over two miles, no one expected her to be primed today for her comeback race. In spite of the 29 percent tax on winnings, she was 35-1, in a fourteen-horse field.

I next introduced Vince to pace handicapping. The narrative comments below the past races of most of the contestants were things like "remained in back of the pack at the outset," or, "slow to gain best stride." This was a field of primarily come-from-behinders at longer distances. Yet, La Coiffeuse had been a front runner, even in her mile Saint-Cloud victory nearly two years ago. Today it looked like she would have the lead all to herself.

And so she did. Down the long backstretch, she loped along ahead of the pack. Half way through the race, at the hairpin turn into the stretch, the horses that were trying to make up ground all went very wide.

But the most grueling part, the slightly uphill stretch, was still to come. Rarely do you see a front runner hold on over the heavy Saint-Cloud green. At 35-1 I would have been delighted if La Coiffeuse had lasted for place. That was defeatist thinking. No horse could even make a run at her. She had conserved her energy early and was left with all the late energy required.

Vince was ecstatic. We went in to collect at the mutuel windows next to the cafe-bar. A sleek woman was perched on a bar stool as if she were modeling for a lusting Rodin.

"Hey, she's beautiful but I'm getting off better with this!" Vince winked, holding up the winning ticket.

He wanted to stay for more. I explained to him that La Coiffeuse was the only "transvestite" of the day. In handicapping, we want horses that look like one thing but are secretly something else. La Coiffeuse was packaged as a jumper but had a hidden identity for the opposite genre on the flat.

Handicapping in France, I told Vince, requires lots of study in order to uncover infrequent betting opportunities. The passion that was supposed to replace his sex addiction would have to come primarily in the research, only partially in the betting.

A week passed and I began to think I had pulled off another Willy. Vince would be playing Brahms, with a *Paris-Turf* under his violin case, and all was serene.

But then one day, Vince did not show up. With no gig, I went out to Longchamps to make up the difference. I barely broke even, though, and then only when my horse that had placed was moved up on a disqualification.

After cashing my ticket, I hopped a train and went directly to Vince's apartment, nearly tripping on the miniature steps that spiraled up to it. When Dominique opened the door, I could see she had been crying. With no makeup to smudge, her reddened eyes were the primary sign of distress. Outwardly I saw nothing kinky about her, nothing that would have made her the choice of a sex addict like Vince.

Whatever had happened, I figured Vince was to blame. I had seen him in action on the bus. As is often the case, my analysis of human nature was wrong. Turned out that Dominique had initiated the trouble.

"He was spending all his time studying the races," she told me, indignantly, with an array of hand gestures more foreign than the language itself. "Vincent was so wrapped up in it that I had to get angry with him. What else could I do?"

She spoke with a beautiful French accent, stressing the second syllable, "Vin*cent*", nasalized "n" and silent "t".

I could see a patch-up job was urgently needed. It wouldn't take many arguments in his marriage to trigger a binge in Vince, and with that, my safety net would be gone.

Without asking permission, I picked up Dominique's phone and called Sonia, who had just gotten back from Maison de Victor Hugo.

"I'm calling from Vince's house. Has he phoned?"

"I just got in."

"I'm coming over there with Dominique. We'll leave a message for Vince to catch up with us. I'll bring a *poulet roti*."

"You sound edgy," she said.

"Nothing to worry about. We'll be there in fifteen minutes."

Meanwhile, I tried to come up with some words of wisdom for Dominique but none were forthcoming. We walked in silence. I wanted to apologize but clearly it wasn't my place to tell her why Vince had become a horse racing addict.

We passed Place de la Reunion, where a squatters' community was protesting the ancient neighborhood's high-rise gentrification. A man in big boots who was handing out leaflets stopped to embrace Dominique. "Don't miss the meeting tomorrow night," he told her.

The door to our staircase was at the end of the courtyard, just past a drain that I had covered up with a heavy bricks so that the rats could not scamper out. On the way up the dank staircase, I was hoping Sonia's wisdom would be of help with Dominique and Vincent.

Sonia kissed me, then kissed Dominique, once on the left cheek, then on the right cheek, then once again on both sides.

Alone I knew I couldn't keep Vince and Dominique together. If anyone could mediate successfully between them, it would be Sonia.

Sonia and Dominique had met only once, when we had eaten out, the four of us and Deedee, at a cheap bistro around the corner. Dominique had dished out her Trotskyite ideology. Sonia, in her special way, had brought the conversation back down to earth with one simple statement.

"I agree with your goals," she had said, "but people have to change themselves from within before they can change the world."

Sonia's social philosophy happened to coincide with my racing philosophy. The "correct" race analysis alone cannot make a winner. The player has to be transformed from within. A system, for ponies or politics, may look good on paper but if imposed from above, it is destined to fail.

The three of us began to eat without Vince but I was not hungry. I had visions of Vince being tossed off the hill of Montmartre by an angry pimp, bumping down one of its winding staircases.

A few minutes past eight o'clock, Vince called. He sounded exhausted. He'd seen my message and said he'd be over in ten minutes. I wanted to ask him where he had been, but that would have to wait for a private moment.

When he walked in, I looked for some sign in his angular face that would tell me if he'd gone on a sex binge. There was no hint. Then again, addicts are good at hiding their problem.

"Bonsoir, Dominique," was his formal acknowledgment of his wife's presence.

Sonia invited Vince to some chicken. He was about as hungry as I was, enough for one bite.

"Sorry I couldn't make it to Chatelet, Matt. No way I could call. We don't have a business phone in the Metro, do we?"

Sonia waited until everyone had settled. She knew how to wait, another important horseplayer characteristic. Too bad she didn't play the ponies.

"Dominique," she said. "Why were you were so upset this morning?"

"Like I said. Vin*cent* spends all his time studying the racing paper. Like a fanatic."

I prayed that Vince wouldn't counterattack with a jab against her Trotskyite politics. Put both sides on the defensive and there would be no chance of establishing a common ground.

I looked at Vince. He looked back, as if to plead, "What can I tell her, that I'm a sex addict who's in racing as therapy?"

Sonia smiled.

"Dominique, you know Matt is a horse race fanatic, too. And I love that!"

"How can you love it when your husband goes for hours without acknowledging your presence," Dominique retorted.

"For Matt, horse racing is the Other Woman. It's another passion in his life that keeps his spirits positive. I don't mind sharing him with racing when it keeps him happy and he makes a few dollars."

The afternoon light came through the open shutters, highlighting Sonia's smooth olive complexion. Contrasted with Dominique's expressive gestures was Sonia's restraint. Only the sensorial wisdom in her eyes added force to her words.

Dominique was trained for listening to abstract analysis. She seemed to respond to Sonia's arguments. It was the kind of dialectical reasoning she was accustomed to. For the rest of the evening, the Other-Woman argument seemed to work and they left in good spirits.

But the next morning, Vince didn't show up for our usual gig. I watched the people rush by in both directions. Many of the men wore business suits. At the other end of the spectrum were the hippie anachronisms. There was a whole society down there. Curiously, it was the less affluent ones who usually tossed us a coin. One of our regular contributors, a tall, wiry African man, walked by, said "bonjour" and disappeared into the crowd.

I couldn't help wondering why at this juncture of my life, my destiny was tethered to a guy like Vince. Miles Davis could afford to not show up for an engagement; but Vince was no Miles Davis. My alternative was the races. Today the jumpers were scheduled at Auteuil. They tended to run more formfully than the flats. Once in awhile you could find a lone front runner that controlled the pace but there were none on the day's card.

I looked up the stairway toward the Pont Neuilly line, hoping to see Vince hurrying down. He wasn't. Meanwhile, Marie hopefully tuned her viola. One of the panhandling drunks who hangs out in the Porte D'Orleans station liked her sound and dropped a twenty-cent coin into her case.

A half hour later, I was ready to give up. I had met Vince in a bar. After the races, I would look for a bar where musicians hung out and maybe find another gig.

I was about to pack up my clarinet when Vince emerged from the crowd.

"Goddamnit, where the hell have you been?" I barked.

"Dominique and me, we were in the middle of something, you know, we had to play the last movement," he winked.

While he tuned his violin, I confronted him.

"Tell me the truth. Where were you yesterday after your argument with Dominique?"

"Don't worry, Matt. I took a stack of *Paris-Turfs* to the Saint-Blaise library. That was the best way for me to calm down. I was handicapping and doing research. I think I've come up with something. What you call a transvestite. It's running in today's sixth. He's a flat runner, trying the hurdles for the first time. Lemme see what you think."

GURU

I no longer believe that the shortest distance between two points is a straight line. I had gone from L.A. to D.C. by way of Paris, where I'd met Roland at a jam session. With Roland's piano player splitting to form another group, I sat in to fill a void at a concert at La Villette. One thing led to another and here I was ten minutes from the Lincoln Memorial doing gigs with one of the craftiest sax players around.

As usual, my night work left me time to bet the horses most afternoons. In theory, I was ideally positioned to become a professional player. The scared-money syndrome was now eliminated with the steady gigs. A new OTB restaurant, The Cracked Claw, had opened up in nearby Frederick County, offering a menu of four tracks to play. I could cherry pick my specialty races and still get enough volume of action to make some meaningful money.

But the year in Paris had left me rusty. I was not readjusting to American racing, which was undergoing changes of its own. There were smaller fields, leaving fewer decent payoffs. And much of the information that had been part of my private research was now being published in the revamped Daily Racing Form, making it far less valuable on the toteboard.

So I was spending afternoons at the OTB trying to reeducate myself, looking for a new edge. I had always laughed at how some of the most confident movers and shakers of the professional world were reduced to infantile dependency when groping for a good bet at the track. Now, I too was among them, and it wasn't funny anymore. I'd lost sixteen straight bets.

I looked up from my table and scanned the monitors. Nothing in particular stood out. Looking back down, I thought I caught a glimpse of a person who should have been three thousand miles away. I rubbed my eyes. It was him.

Russ Andrews in Frederick County! It didn't make sense. Horseplayers traveled to California from all parts of the country to attend a Russ Andrews seminar. They went to him. And now, he had come to me. And just in time, just when everything about horse racing seemed to operate by a new set of vague rules known only to a privileged few. I was not among the privileged.

So remote was our little OTB nestled in the green rolling hills of upcounty that none of the locals recognized Andrews. But I recognized him. His southern California sun tan stood out in this late November, reminding me of subdued, mellow afternoons at Santa Anita. Our sun was only there out of some tedious tradition, a distant memory. If you looked hard enough through the frosted windows, you could see an occasional snow flurry.

Andrews was the only guy in the place with a laptop computer. He was the only patron who asked for wine instead of beer. The waitress didn't even know what wines they had on the menu. He asked her to find out what they had from California, said that the recent crops of French wines couldn't match the best California ones.

I had actually been considering flying out to Arcadia, California for an Andrews weekend seminar. I'd read his books. He was a true legend. Two hundred dollars was a small bet for him. A thousand was more like it. He made a six-figure income from the horses. That was what I explained to Sonia when I considered going out there.

"What do you need a seminar for?" she asked. "You already win at the races."

"Lately," I told her, "none of my methods are paying their way. The game has changed and I've got to change with it."

Sonia figured that most guys who play the horses are losers. She had seen me win enough so that one difficult readjustment period hardly mattered. She still expected that my fortunes would inevitably turn in an upward direction. It was hard for her to understand that a normal slump can become permanent if self-confidence has been lost. My confidence had been left behind at Longchamps and the M section of the Santa Anita grandstand.

Sonia saw it from a practical, financial point of view.

"How long will it take you to win back the three hundred for the seminar, another five hundred for the air fare and another two hundred for the hotel? And that's not counting what you'll lose by skipping your gigs."

One year in Paris had done Sonia a world of good. She hardly looked like the frazzled woman who had once held a high-powered position in a big bank. Now in her mid-thirties, she bounced around like a high school kid. With a meaningful decision at stake, however, her demeanor would suddenly turn sharp and purposeful.

My ex, Brenda, had become so irrational that I'd stopped paying attention to her. But there was no getting around Sonia. With her, the roles were reversed. It was my man's intuition in dialogue with her objective analysis. But apart from a few tactical disagreements, she was on my side. Not like Brenda, who had made public statements to the effect that I was essentially an enemy of work because I did things that had the word "play" in them. Play music. Play horses.

Sonia smiled faintly.

"What about those racing books you returned to Andrews? Did you ever get your refund?"

Shit, she remembered everything. I had ordered a couple hundred dollars worth of handicapping books from Andrews' Los Angeles store. Some of the books turned out to be the same old horseshit, not the ones by Andrews, of course. I returned the bad ones, requesting my guaranteed money back refund. I never got it.

I called him. He told me he'd sent me the refund, that it must have been lost in the mail. He was sorry. He'd tell his bookkeeper to send another check. I never got it. It was only forty-six bucks. I figured he was so busy with his horse betting that he forgot to follow up. I had to forgive him for that because I was the same way with my music. When given the choice between banging out a new arrangement or some menial task, my passion pushed my obligation aside. I figured I had this in common with Andrews.

Besides, Andrews lifestyle intrigued me. I'd read everything he had ever written. I knew his modus operandi. He would wake up early to do his Inside Voice radio program, giving out the scratches and interviewing handicappers and trainers. Then he'd go through his second phase of handicapping and get out to the track. After the races, he'd compile his research, track profile, trainer and jockey stats, and other more esoteric angles. Later in the evening he'd record the day's races on his VCR and do his preliminary analysis of the next day's card.

With a lifestyle like that one, who's going to worry about promptly paying electric bills or refund requests. In my case, I had Sonia to remind me to take care of business.

But the freedom I gained from Sonia taking over the financial busywork came in exchange for her veto power on the family budget. I needed to come up with a long-range strategy that would compensate for the short-term expense of a seminar.

"Look baby, the way I learned the keyboard was to stalk guys like Herbie Hancock and Harold Mayburn. Where would my chops be today if I hadn't followed Wayne Shorter from city to city."

"It's not analogous," she fired back.

"Sure it is. Jazz and horse betting. Both swing, in their own way of course, and both involve improvisation. You don't learn to improvise from a book. You watch how it's done. It's like auto mechanics. You don't learn from the manual. You learn from someone who shows you what to do.

"Fine," she said, "but what if you choose the wrong master. Andrews didn't even send you your refund!"

"He's just absent-minded, like other brilliant people. Like Einstein might wear two different shoes. Something like that."

I called Phil, my agent. Asked if he could get me a gig in L.A., my old stomping grounds, the same weekend as the Andrews seminar. The gig never materialized.

Since Sonia was not a player, she couldn't understand that in horse betting, being there on the scene is different from book knowledge. She was one of those rare species that learned computers through the manual. "Why can't you simply learn it from the book?" she asked.

I needed to hang around Andrews and see how he made his decisions. Same way I followed Hancock around, in order to loosen up my keyboard technique. Choosing the precise chord is no different form making a betting decision. You've got to get beyond the surface of the melody to unlock the good stuff. Good handicappers lose money if they don't follow up their race analysis with the right betting moves. I figured if you want to be a winner, hang out with winners.

And now, I wouldn't have to go to California. Andrews was here. I considered walking over to his table and offering two hundred for a day-long session, right there in the off-track betting restaurant. Maybe after an hour or two, I could remind him about the forty-six bucks.

I thought about what Sonia, my financial advisor, would say, if she knew. Take that two hundred, she'd say, and put it on the favorite in the feature, to show. Just like the venerable gambling expert Scarne had written. When we hooked up together, it was Sonia who got me out of debt. She had earned my respect. But her knowledge of horse racing was limited. I had always looked at show betting as a defeatist measure.

The bridgejumpers, they put thousands to show on a sure bet. They make what seems to be a puny bit of money. But two thousand that wins you a hundred dollars in one minute and eleven seconds is better than any bank account could do.

We're talking about sure bets, mind you. John Henry, Spectacular Bid, Sunday Silence.

You can be a longshot player, but when you're mired in a losing streak, as I was, the prospect of walking up to the window and collecting at $2.40 becomes tempting. The way things were at the moment, the clerks would see me approaching and they would know it was to bet, not to collect.

Fortunately, I now had an alternative. Russ Andrews was here. I looked over to his table and planned my strategy. I realized there was no need to talk to Andrews. I could do a Herbie Hancock on him. All I had to do was follow him around. He was a half foot taller than me, so I'd be lost in the crowd. I left my Brooklyn Dodgers baseball hat in the sleave of my coat so that I would not stand out. Thankfully, a few days earlier, I had shaved off the beard I'd grown in Paris. I looked like one of the crowd.

I'd be right behind him. Every time he stepped up to the betting counter, I would listen carefully to exactly what he was betting, then check back in my racing form. I'd see how he managed his money, and exactly what kind of horses he bet.

"What do you see in that horse," I might spring on him later in the afternoon. He had a reputation for giving straight answers. I'd get a seventeen-syllable piece of wisdom. But by the time I was ready to ask him a question, I'd probably know the answer already. Besides, a man's actions say more than his words.

I'd also get to see how he reacted to winning. And maybe to losing, although the legend was that he rarely failed to collect. The word was that Andrews had once been the head of a Fortune 500 company but had gotten bored with the easy money. He wanted to make his living the hard way. He wanted to prove something.

I watched him as he sipped his wine and extracted data from his little desktop toy. The first several races were now part of oblivion, at Aqueduct, Laurel and Calder, and he still hadn't made a bet. Hollywood Park would be beamed in over the wall monitors beginning at 3:30.

One of the qualities of a professional bettor had already shown through. Andrews wasn't hungry for action. Occasionally he'd look up at the OTB regulars as they rushed to make a bet or as they shouted for the seven-horse or the three to get up in time in the stretch. But the people around him were like old wallpaper or elevator music. They were hardly worth noticing.

By the time Andrews left his table, I had gotten past the foam of my third beer. I followed him, out of the no-smoking room, through the crowd. He was in Fred's line. Fred was the slowest of all the mutuel clerks. I waited behind Andrews.

I considered saying, "hey Russ, you could get shut out in Fred's line." That would make me his ally. But it was too early for direct communication. Anonymity was my best tactic.

"Laurel, fourth race, one hundred to win on number six, please."

He left old Fred's counter. Rather than returning to his table, he went three clerks down, to Ray, my regular clerk. Here the line moved faster. I was right behind him.

"Laurel, fourth race, one hundred to win on number six, please."

So that was it! He didn't want to draw attention to his bets. I walked up to Ray, asked for fifty to win on the six. Andrews had bet a Leatherbury horse that was shortening up from a route to seven furlongs. Sneaky move. Toughest move in racing. Horses used to the slow pace of a longer race have trouble keeping up in a sprint. That's what Andrews himself had written in his second book. Now he was contradicting his own advice.

But that was part of his genius. He knew when to break the rules.

The six laid back in mid-pack. I watched Andrews from my table. He didn't stand up, didn't say a word, even took a slow sip of his wine as they went down the backstretch. His classic serenity and stern cheek bones qualified him for a place on Mount Rushmore. The six moved up on the turn, three wide, and drew off to win at 5-2. Still no sign of emotion on Andrew's face. No rush to get up and collect, either. He was a pro. I wanted to emulate him, not necessarily his handicapping but his winning ways.

When Andrews got up to take a leak, I was there too, in the next urinal. What would Sonia say if she knew I was readjusting my urinating schedule to conform to Andrews'?

Andrews' next bet was $500 to show on a maiden claimer at Hollywood Park. One hundred fifty here, one fifty there, and another two hundred with a third mutuel clerk, chain-smoking Elvira. The maiden was trained by McAnally, the only class dropper in the race. He'd finished in the money at the Maiden Special Weight level. The rest of the horses had all already lost at the cheaper 32,000 level.

Two things I noticed. He checked the toteboard, meticulously. With a hand-held calculator, he was appraising the potential show payoffs. I could tell it was a place-show calculation since he did it only when the wall monitors switched to the columns that display how much money is on each horse in the win, place and show pools.

He also watched the horses in the paddock and post parade, as well as one could on a TV monitor. The McAnally horse looked great. Shiny, prancing, tail up, not a bit washy.

I made another bet, copying Andrews in everything but size of bet.

The McAnally horse broke into the lead and never looked back. He paid $2.40 to show. Andrews had just made a hundred bucks. He made it look easy. I considered all the changes I'd have to make in my personality in order to bet like him. Think big. I needed to think big. Like Sonia argued, I shouldn't even be working the clubs in Adams-Morgan anymore. I should be playing larger auditoriums like the Hollywood Bowl. I only needed to think big. That's what Sonia said.

Then there was the matter of emotions. Andrews got no visible thrill from making wagers. He was all business. I would have to give up my lust for this game, treat it like accounting or claims adjustment.

I let Andrews out of my view in order to call Sonia from a phone in the lobby. I told her I was on to something big, that I wouldn't make it back for dinner, that I'd explain later.

Luckily, Andrews had not left his perch. I ordered a grilled hamburger with fries and another beer. Each time Andrews got up, I followed. But each of these little excursions led to nothing. Andrews would wait for the place and show pools to flash on the monitor, press buttons on his calculator, then come back to his table with no bet. If you start at point A and return to the exact same point, the physics formula says that you haven't done any work at all. In Andrews' case, the formula was wrong.

With a late scratch, the feature at Hollywood Park was shaved down to a five-horse field. Apparently an unbettable race. One filly stood out, Eliza, ridden by Chris McCarron. A proven grade I winner against four allowance horses.

To my surprise, Andrews got up. He left the calculator on the table. Surely he knew ahead of time that Eliza would pay the minimum $2.10 to show. The only feasible bet might have been a one-way exacta, if you thought that the longest shot on the board had a chance for second.

I followed him to the betting counter. The nemesis of all horseplayers is the sure-bet whose odds are too low. I decided to back away a bit, moving over to another line, parallel to the one where Russ Andrews stood. I risked finding myself out of hearing range when Andrews called out his bet. But the man had a clear voice. He was a radio personality and a seminar specialist.

"Four hundred to show on the three."

The three was Eliza. It made no sense! Maybe Eliza had about a 99.5 percent chance to finish first, second or third in this five-horse field. But was Andrews willing to take ten cents profit for each two dollars bet?

He got back on another line. Again, four hundred. And another. Four hundred more on Eliza. By the time he'd gone to the fifth clerk, Andrews had dumped two thou on Eliza to show. So, among his specialties, he was a high-priced bridgejumper.

And that left me with seven minutes to decide whether or not I wanted to continue emulating Russ Andrews, whether or not I wanted to become a bridgejumper myself. All five public handicappers had Eliza on top in bold print: their best bet of the day. The several decent stakes fillies that could have challenged this daughter of Mt. Livermore and sister of Housebuster, had defected from this race in order to look for easier pickings.

My private seminar had become a test of my true class. Was I ready for the major leagues, or was I just a smalltimer with illusions of grandeur?

But then again, I had to ask myself why a pro like Andrews would make a bet like this. Was there something going on in his life I didn't know about? Why was he here and not in California?

I figured I needed to put down at least five hundred in order to rate a place in Andrews' league. If I was going to open any direct communication with him, I had this job to do first. Five hundred to make twenty-five bucks! My friend Sal once attended an Andrews seminar. Said Andrews had collected on all seven bets for the weekend. "The guy's invincible!" he marveled.

On most days, I wouldn't even have five hundred in my pocket. But I'd collected twice now, thanks to Andrews, and that had built me up to five crisp ones in my left front pocket. It was two minutes to post. I pulled them out and laid them on the counter.

I felt as if all my one hundred fifty pounds had suddenly been sent in as a blocking back against a 300-pound Minnesota Vikings pass rusher.

"Five hundred to show on the three."

Never before had I bet so much on a single horse. My mind was reeling out of focus. Strange images were storming through my brain. A dissonant counterpoint was weaving in and out of the melody. The simple tune said Eliza all the way. But in the counterpoint was the moving image of Lady's Secret, the invincible Lady's Secret, 2-5 at Belmont, five horse field, as she bolted the rail. The end of a brilliant career. They had asked too much of her. She had said "enough."

There's got to be some dissonance if the music is going to get down to the gut. No dissonance is what happens to Mexican food when a chain restaurant gets a hold of it. Eliza was a bland bet. A dumb melody like the one you hear at Disneyland, the one that says "it's a small world," again and again. Stupid dolls telling us it's a small world.

"Wait," I said. "Cancel that. Make that two dollars to show on number one, two to show on the two-horse, two to show on the four, and two more on number five, to show."

I gave Ray a hundred, got back ninety-two. The image of the 2-5 Lady's Secret bolting over the rail had gotten me into a dissonant mode, symmetrically the opposite of my guru's. He had bet a lot; I bet a little. He went for a sure bet; I risked a little for a potentially outlandish payoff. He bet with his head; a surreal vision had led to my bet.

Eliza took the lead. One of the other horses, a sprinter stretching out, decided to press the pace, wrestling the lead from Eliza. McCarron could have eased back. But he didn't. He did what many jocks do on invincible horses. He disregarded the pace, figuring Eliza would win no matter what tactics she used.

And there was Eliza, in a pace duel with a cheap allowance horse. With Eliza on the inside, the duel would carry the rival wide on the turn. Surely Eliza would put away the cheap speed horse. My eight dollars meant nothing. I expected Andrews to collect. I would get back $4.20 . He would win another easy hundred.

But no matter how much McCarron asked of her, Eliza failed to draw clear of her rival. I remembered the one big dissonant chord that opens the last movement of Beethoven's Ninth, the one that brings the whole history of music to a new, sublime level. Everything familiar to horse race handicapping was now shifting to a new level. Eliza, along with her running companion, began to shorten stride. The soloist was done for it and the chorus was taking over. I looked at Andrews. No change of expression. Square and stony like an old Dick Tracy cartoon face.

Three horses swept by the two duelers. Eliza was out of the money. The fact that her more than nine tenths of the show pool was to be distributed amongst the other show bettors meant I was going to pick up three extraordinary show payoffs.

The board lit up. All three of my show prices exceeded $30 bucks. For my eight-dollar investment, I would collect more than a hundred.

But there was no time to think of collecting. Andrews was packing up his laptop, leaving a tip, putting on his overcoat.

Maybe nobody's an authority in this game, I thought. Still, I latched on to one last bit of evidence, trying to revive the image of Andrews as a true pro. Any other player would have stayed around for the last race to play catchup. Not him. It was virtually the same expression he had when his 5-2 shot had won the fourth at Laurel, although I had detected some reddening in his cheeks.

Andrews walked out the door, into the windy night. I decided to stick around and take a stab at the ninth race trifecta.

WAITING FOR STANDRIDGE

During the winter months, with most turf racing in hibernation, I was picking and choosing my spots, rarely finding a prime bet. Somehow, though, the realization that I was just fine without a guru allowed me to make a string of right decisions I'd have surely butchered in my more negative periods.

I had purchased a volume of research on Gulfstream. Most of it was helpful for the daily grind but I could only isolate one piece of information that might lead to a major score. A lesser known trainer by the name of Steve Standridge was shown to be a specialist in bringing horses from a layoff to win first time back. The profit if you bet all his comeback horses was greater than 200 percent, "enough to make you cream in your pants," Wilson Tripp would have said.

This was a rare occasion when a trainer has both a high return on investment and a high hit rate. Most players were not going to take this guy too seriously though since the sample was not large. Even if the public were made aware of Standridge's talent, they were unlikely to bet him down from his twenty-dollar average mutuel.

Halfway through January, no Standridge layoff horses had materialized. While I was making a profit at the OTB, on a dollars-per-hour basis, I might as well have been working at McDonalds. On most days, the only dramatic action was the daily ice and sleet storm.

Inside the Cracked Claw Restaurant, we got a more extended taste of winter. At Gulfstream, each time I found a good turf race, it was taken off the grass because of a thunderstorm. Meanwhile, Santa Anita was getting hit with such heavy rains that fields were often reduced to five, even four horses. With my longshot trainers Blengs, Tagg and Capuano taking off to warmer venues, my home-track Laurel past performances took on the look of the enigmatic facade of a Mayan temple.

None of this bothered me. It would only take one Standridge horse to make my winter. The first one came in mid-January, in a six-furlong claiming race. He went off at 22-1 in spite of my hundred dollar bet. Off a bit slowly, he moved up along the rail to become the third horse in a pace duel. He had the lead in mid-stretch, only to get passed by two horses and finish third by a half length.

I considered my hundred dollars well spent. Only a half length had separated me from $2,300. I now knew that Standridge was for real. If I ever decided to run cross country again after my twenty-year layoff, I'd ask him to help get me back into shape.

Each morning I would drive, sometimes it was more like ski, to the news store for the Form. My ritual involved opening it up to Gulfstream and scanning the pages for Standridge. If his name came up, I'd then immediately check if his horse had been laid off at least a month and a half.

During the next two weeks, it was a question of which would come out first, the sun or a Standridge layoff horse. Neither had made an appearance.

By now, I had friends waiting with me for Standridge. Grabowski and I spoke over the phone on particular mornings when a bettable race popped up. His counter-attack betting style came from his soccer playing days. He would let things happen and avoid conflict until a clear opening materialized, then strike with all he had. Grabowski would only bet when he knew something that the crowd was not privy to. A part of his income was derived from free lance writing but most of it came from the track.

"Don't worry Matt," he consoled me. "Wait and win. That's the system."

I remembered my college hitchhiking days. The rule was: the longer the wait, the better the ride.

Often I'd wake up in the middle of the night to the unexpected blast of the heater and mentally raise my potential bet a few hundred. In the morning, I'd wonder what had made me so bold and would lower it, but never back to the original hundred. This night-morning pendulum continued until my morning bet was up to three hundred.

Finally, in the second week of February, Standridge arrived. He was entering a three-year-old filly by the name of My Molly. She had raced once as a two-year old and had hardly run a lick. Now she was coming back in another maiden special weight, stretching out to a route. She would be running on the next day's card in the third race.

Grabowski told me he had to be out of town. Town for him was in Massachusetts, where all the tracks offered simulcasting from Gulfstream. I had never met him in person but we trusted one another to the extent that we took turns putting in each other's action. If I had an out-of-town gig, he did the same for me.

"Can you spot me two hundred on the Standridge horse?" he asked.

"Sure can," I said.

"Shall we set some odds parameters," he asked. "We need at least four to one."

"Don't worry," I assured him. "Sweep has her at thirty and no one mentions her in the consensus."

That night the sky turned into an ice cube machine. Sonia heard the crunching against the roof and woke up scared.

"I think I'll put four hundred on My Molly," I told her.

Clearly, Sonia and I were thinking about different subjects. But in the morning, our two themes converged when I discovered that I was going to have to chop away the ice from my car. Schools were closed again, for the fourth day in the last two weeks, so Deedee was out there trying to help me scrape the ice.

By 11:30, I had gotten the windows clear and the ice shoveled from around my tires. I'd still have to skate the car out of the residential streets in order to get it to the freeway.

"Is one horse worth risking your life?" Sonia asked.

"Most days the answer's no," I laughed. "But this is a Standridge layoff horse. I've been waiting for Standridge the whole winter. I gotta go."

Once I coaxed the car onto Route 355, the road was passable. But sleet began to fall again. The defroster couldn't keep up with it. I navigated by looking through a small porthole on the windshield.

Fortunately, on the freeway, traffic was moving at only 35 miles per hour. The incessant sleet had created a porthole effect on all the cars. Maybe the ice storm was a message for me not to bet. How foolish it would be, risking my life to lose four hundred dollars.

I decided to lower my bet to two hundred. At an estimated 20-1, I'd collect $4,000. Four thousand dollars plus a safe return home would be a double triumph.

My timing was perfect. I was arriving about a half hour before post. I didn't want to wait around the OTB while the ice piled up outside. I would leave as soon as they ran the race.

I got off the freeway at Urbana, skidding down the offramp. I drove up to the OTB and my first reaction was, Hey, only three cars here. The players were brave with a bet but cowardly in the ice. I walked up to the door and saw the sign:

Racing and simulcasting canceled due to weather.

What a fool! It hadn't occurred to me to phone Laurel to make sure they were open. They hadn't closed down for any of the other recent ice storms. How could I imagine they would shut down precisely on Standridge's day?

Of course it wasn't snowing in southern Florida, where My Molly was going to run. I considered phoning Las Vegas from a booth to get a friend to put in my bet. But it was too late. Even if one of my friends were not in a race book by now, it was too close to post time for him to leave the house and get over there.

My anger bordered on self-hatred. All this time waiting for Standridge and I hadn't planned for extenuating circumstances. There was another possibility. The ice storm was there for a purpose, to save me two hundred bucks.

Driving back, looking through the diminishing porthole, my concerns now shifted to getting back alive. I passed a jackknifed semi and racing became a remote snow drift in my subconscious.

Back in my neighborhood, I had trouble getting the car up the incline that led to our block. When it finally spurted over the top, my grip on the steering wheel was so tight that it was a chore to unlock my knuckles.

I went into the house, not as a horseplayer but as a family man. I hugged Sonia and Deedee as if I hadn't seen them in years.

"You were right," I said to Sonia. "I shouldn't have risked my life."

"How much did you lose?" she asked.

Before I could answer, the phone was ringing. I picked up the receiver. It was Grabowski, calling from somewhere in New York City.

I tried to tell him about the aborted wager. But he had something pressing to say that wouldn't wait.

"I phoned the Gulfstream results line. We won."

"You mean the Standridge filly," I said, wishing it were something else. Depression welled up in me like an inner tundra. "How much did he pay?"

Grabowski could tell there was something wrong.

"Matt, don't tell me you didn't get it down!"

"The track and OTBs were closed," I said, "because of the ice storm."

A lesser friend would have doubted me, suspecting that just maybe I had decided to keep the profit for myself.

"He paid eighty-five," Gabowski said. "Eighty-five bucks!"

I did a few quick calculations. The ice storm had cost us each $8,500.

Grabowski seemed to take it better than I did. He said something about circumstances beyond our control. Sensing that I was losing it, he offered a bit of advice.

"Matt, don't let this lead to clinical depression."

I imagined a warm smile on a face I had never seen.

My first impulse was to take it out on Sonia and Deedee. Or maybe on myself. One phone call to Laurel and I would have known enough to get my action in through friends in Las Vegas.

I went outside to work out my anger against its source. I began shoveling the ice off the walk.

There was only one thing to do: continue waiting for Standridge.

THIRD CHOICE

After catching a thirty-five buck Standridge layoff winner, I approached the game with renewed confidence and went on a winning streak. In fact, I was up over three grand for the Laurel meet when my betting, as inevitably happens to every horseplayer, turned cold again. Recognizing the symptoms early, I scaled back on my bets, played fewer races in order to weather the slump. It wasn't so much bad handicapping. My horses were in the money, usually at high odds, but they just couldn't seem to hold on during a speed duel or quite get up from off the pace.

Fortunately, I discovered an ally at about the same time in the form of Kristin Wood, the public handicapper for the *Maryland Sentinel*. What I noticed while reading her daily comments was that she was particularly adept at identifying legitimate longshots, though she often downplayed them by listing them as her third pick.

On any given day at Laurel Race Course, however, it was not unusual to overhear the hard-core regulars discussing her column in sexist terms and concluding that someone else on the *Sentinel* staff must be doing her picks. They would behold her pretty face and come to that conclusion, especially when her top choice came in at 6-1. But if Wood's Best Bet ran off the board, these same players would change their tune. Then it was *her* pick, after all, and one of them would invariably suggest she got the job by sleeping with the *Sentinel's* board of directors.

Anyhow, one warm spring afternoon during this time, I was hanging out at the far end of the rail, near the turn for home, to keep away from the distracting chatter of the regulars, when Jake spotted me and lumbered over. I could already hear his voice deja vu when he chirped,

"Hey Matt, where you been? Come on, who do ya like here?"

I flashed my *Sentinel* and pointed to Kristin Wood's selections.

"I'm following *her* lately," I rubbed it in a little. "I can't pick my nose, but if you tally up her picks for the last month, she's showing an eighteen percent profit."

That was my helpful hint. If Jake wanted to be a whodoyaliker, he could curb his prejudice and have Kristin every race for twenty-five cents in the *Sentinel*.

Besides, I wasn't in the mood to discuss the races. My old nemesis, the scared-money syndrome was back again, only with a different twist. While my previous bouts with it had been primarily the result of external economic distress, this battle was far more serious because it came from within. Even though I had improved my game, I knew I still wasn't playing boldly enough and it was costing me.

The previous day's fifth race typified my dilemma. In a maiden turf event, I had isolated two horses that had never tried the green and were bred to love it, Turkish Tryst and Seulement. I bet them both to win and boxed them in the exacta. I had seventy bucks on the line.

For an extra sixteen dollars, I had planned to wheel some insurance trifectas, Turkish Tryst-All-Seulement and Seulement-All-Turkish Tryst, just in case my exacta finished first-third. The strategy would have been considered outlandish by most players, but to me it seemed sensible enough.

First-third exacta finishes are among the most frustrating outcomes in racing. By using "all" horses in the place hole of a trifecta, should a 99-1 shot split my exacta, the tri payoff would explode the tote.

Some undefined sentiment had prevented me from putting in that extra bet. It was not something as obviously debilitating as worrying about the rent money. It was a faint but firm voice from within that told me the bet was foolish and immoral. To include horses I had already eliminated from contention was degenerate gambling.

The 10-1 Turkish Tryst won the race with Seulement finishing third. As it was, the betting favorite Short Suspenders was the one that finished second and ruined my exacta. But even with the public choice squeezed in there, the tri came back at eight hundred bucks. Even though I had won a hundred fifty on the race, I felt worse than if I had lost. Big scores were eluding me because I was unwilling to bet in a kinkier way.

My imagination was intact, but the courage to act on it was being throttled by some mysterious force. At my night club gigs, a similar phenomenon was stifling my solos. The unique keyboard style I'd been on the verge of consolidating kept eluding me. Even though Roland, the sax player, sensed a breakthrough and encouraged me, I just couldn't quite let go.

Meanwhile, back at the Laurel rail, Jake snorted in response to my touting Kristin Wood's picks.

"Since when you listen to what a broad's got to say in the paper. Look here, she's got the Cartwright horse on top at 8-1. I don't see a damn thing in that horse."

"Good for her," I said, "Most public handicappers play it safe and go with the chalk."

In the past, I reflected, I'd always done my best when my back was to the wall. Maybe there was a lesson here. When Sonia decided to quit her job to spend more time with our daughter Deedee, I had actually welcomed her challenge to get serious and make more money at the track.

She had been working in insurance, with a company that booked bets. Folks were betting that they would have an auto accident, or that they would die. The company was betting that they wouldn't.

The challenge Sonia hit me with just happened to coincide with the interior conspiracy against my horse betting. I no longer harbored doubts that I could win. But in order to score big, there was still this invisible psychological barrier that was stifling my alternative betting styles.

I was also troubled by my friend Nick's disappearance from the game, as if I were in danger of following in his footsteps. He had withdrawn from racing right after his most successful meet, like Thelonius Monk, who, in the prime of his career, had said good-bye to the Five Spot on the Bowery and then faded away, cloistered in the mansion of his patrons for the last decade of his life.

We all have our half-life. The weaker the atomic particle, the longer its half-life; the most intense particles have the shortest half-life. Monk's disappearance was precipitated by the ultimate intensity of his piano discoveries. Nick's exit from horse betting came after his most passionate attack on the odds. I had been playing the racing game intensely for a long time. I wondered if my own half-life was up.

Jake and I watched the race. The favorite won at 4-5 with Kristin Wood's longshot placing. I figured she had the exacta.

With Nick not around to help me identify my demons, I had brought up the scared-money syndrome with Sonia, mentioning how my decision making might become tainted, knowing that I was obligated to make up for her lost income. As usual, her answer was financially objective:

"Remember Russ Andrews," she said. "He wanted to make a little each time by betting a lot. From what I've seen of your game, it's better to try to make a lot by investing a little. Otherwise, you might as well put your bankroll in a CD. Just begin with smaller amounts. Little by little, you can raise your bet as the bankroll grows."

She should have been a player. She would have had the betting skills, that's for sure. But she was talking as if the neurons that made betting decisions and the ones that transmitted psychological hangups were wired in separate systems. Maybe they were, but with me the wiring was crossed.

I had begun to understand that the scared-money syndrome was laden with complex dualities. On the one hand, it would have been relatively easy to double my bet on the Turkish Tryst race, that is, if I were merely adding the money to conventional bets such as win or exacta. But my inhibition concerned the type and not the amount of the bet. A hundred to win on Turkish Tryst? No problem. Sixteen dollars of weird trifecta combinations? The red light went on.

I considered self-therapy. But in reviewing my past betting history, my quantum leaps usually occurred when dialoguing with other players. Having read Kristin Wood's columns, I realized that she too suffered from a weird duality, by the fact that she would use conventional handicapping for her top two picks while saving her most bizarre riffs for the third spot.

With the sixth race unbettable, I went in under the grandstand for cup of coffee. As is often the case, I saw her mingling with the crowd. This time I decided to talk to her. We had something in common. I wanted to share some of the baggage I was carrying around, but not with someone like Jake.

"Kristin Wood," I said, seeing her up close for the first time. She was at least two inches taller than I was. I groped for the right words. No doubt the players around us thought I was coming on to her. They see a guy walk up to a blond and that's what they imagine. I wanted something more serious. I wanted to tap her mind.

"Thanks for Unknown Hero last week," I said. "It was your third choice but I loved your argument. I never would have had him on my own."

"I lost that race," she said. "I'm terrible at managing my money...Say, haven't we met before?"

"I doubt it. Once in awhile my picture's in the entertainment section of the paper. You might have seen it there."

"Now I remember. You're a musician. I saw you play at The Saloon in Georgetown. You were great."

She was on her way to the Food Fair and invited me to join her. Along the way, she filled me in on how she got started. She had gone to Elmont High School on Long Island, in the shadow of Belmont Park. Her Dad was a racing fan. In her senior year, on her way to becoming valedictorian, she often cut her last tennis class and skipped out to the track to make bets for her P.E. instructor. He was a player and she would take out his action. They had it all arranged with one of the tellers, who would take her bets even though she was underaged.

Following high school, she went to Columbia in a pre-med program. By her junior year, she knew she wanted to be near racing, so she changed her major to journalism, specializing in sports.

During our conversation, she acknowledged that she was sometimes privy to inside information on Maryland racing; part of her job involved talking to trainers. The same guys we knew as tight-lipped trainers would sometimes tip her on a horse in exchange for a little publicity.

I also learned that she was butchering her own selections by doing three-horse exacta boxes and missing out on win overlays with her second and third choices. She was down on herself. She knew she was a good handicapper, but she lacked the betting skills.

We agreed to exchange notes from time to time in the hope that our discussions would lead to a greater understanding of the mysterious inner forces that were conspiring against our betting liberation.

Beneath each new column, Kristin would write the previous day's results. "Three winners and two seconds," or "Two winners and four seconds." While I was making an occasional score by incorporating her third choices, she was undervaluing her insights by relying exclusively on her top choices.

We met informally on a fairly regular basis, usually when we happened to bump into each other. The talk was strictly horses. This time, over a coffee, I related my findings.

"I see you with two personalities. One is correct, formal, you could say inhibited. That's the one that evaluates itself on the basis of top picks. Then there's the other part of you, the uninhibited part. With your top picks, you're simply reading the music. With your third choices, you're improvising with obscure angles."

It was easy to say these things when I was talking about someone else. But I knew that, when it came to inhibitions, I was also talking about myself.

Curiously, she was enslaved to the very conventions prescribed by the male handicapping establishment. Her top two picks were usually generated from the fastest speed figures and other traditions based on the notion that the past continues uniformly into the present. Her third choice usually broke with the conventions, attempting to project change rather than continuity.

My talk about inhibitions triggered a transformation in the protocol of our conversations.

"Matt, maybe I'm pressing," she said. "When I take too many chances in my selections, I can go a day or two without any winners, and then I hear from my editors."

Most of us bought the *Sentinel*, trashed the news and business sections and kept the racing page. A good chunk of that paper's sales came from the racegoers. The way the editors saw it, if Kristin slumped, their business slumped too.

In her own way, Kristin was also the victim of the scared money syndrome. Her job depended on a high percentage of winners. As a result, she was boxed into a routine based on caution. But no one ever makes money at the races by being prudent.

To prove my point, I went over my *Sentinel* results charts and tallied two months of flat-bet returns on Kristin's selections. Her top two choices both came out with a loss. But as I suspected, her third choices, the unbridled ones, were profitable in spite of their lower hit rate. If she could only convince her editors to evaluate her performance on profit rather than hit rate, she'd be liberated to handicap with no boundaries.

Before leaving, I reminded Kristin about her third choices. There was a perplexed look in her eyes.

"There's something kinky about my third choices," she said. "I guess we're all subject to Calvinistic inhibitions, no matter how hard our parents try to raise us otherwise."

From there I drove over to The Saloon, with my third-choice research still on my mind. Two bars into the first song, I decided to try something out. Each time I faced a split-second decision between several harmonic nuances, I'd go with my third choice. I put the third-choice mechanism on automatic pilot.

When I did my solo on "These Foolish Things," I thought, even Ella would be proud of me. Roland responded with a few riffs I'd never heard before. Hal, the drummer, did some broken-up triplets, just like Elvin. The third-choice method was working just fine.

The next day, I walked through the turnstyle at Laurel with new resolve. Scared money was not that mystery it had been twenty-four hours ago. I had identified the enemy within. Knowing who and where it was, I was prepared to dig in and do battle.

Was I going to win my next bet? I now *knew* that one race meant very little in the long-term scheme of things. I just had to trust myself. Let no inhibitions stop me from reaching my potential.

Jake came up and asked me who I liked. And thankfully just then Kristin, who I usually met after the fifth race, spotted me.

"I'm tied up today in interviews," she said, "but I wanted to tell you I have a surprise for you. You'll see tomorrow."

The next day I saw Kristin's surprise. Her *Sentinel* column had a whole new layout. Rather than keeping track of her number of winners, they were doing it right this time, keeping a flat bet record of her best plays of the day.

I checked out her selections. There was no chalk. They could have titled her column "The Uninhibited Kristin Wood." She was taking a big risk. But that's why we love this game.

I was waiting in line to bet the rail horse in the first race. It was a Hubie Hine shipper by the name of Red Tazz. He had won a two-year-old race as a first-time starter. Now he was coming back after a layoff. A long layoff. A red light flashed within. The "forbidden" sign was activated. Red Tazz had been on a long vacation. The Puritan work ethic told me you win by practicing, not by grazing on the farm.

I struggled against this ghost of John Calvin. Red Tazz had proven he could run fresh. He should have been 8-5. But the public was going by his two-year-old speed figure. He was a three-year old now, which meant he was going to run faster. I was getting 7-2. I glanced at the *Sentinel*. Kristin had him on top, too, but that made little impact on the crowd. Most players are conditioned against betting layoff horses.

I dug deep into my pocket. Sonia believed in me. It was now time for me to believe in myself. What a tradeoff: my being here at Laurel instead of Sonia being caged in at an insurance office, writing memos and evaluating claims.

There was no guarantee that I'd make up for her lost salary. But I had the chance to try, and I was taking it. That was what counted.